UNDEAD
AND UNWORTHY

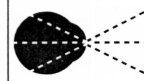

This Large Print Book carries the
Seal of Approval of N.A.V.H.

UNDEAD
AND UNWORTHY

MARYJANICE DAVIDSON

WHEELER PUBLISHING
A part of Gale, Cengage Learning

GALE
CENGAGE Learning

Detroit • New York • San Francisco • New Haven, Conn • Waterville, Maine • London

Copyright © 2008 by MaryJanice Alongi.
Wheeler Publishing, a part of Gale, Cengage Learning.

Wheeler Publishing Large Print Softcover.
The text of this Large Print edition is unabridged.
Other aspects of the book may vary from the original edition.
Set in 16 pt. Plantin.
Printed on permanent paper.

LIBRARY OF CONGRESS CATALOGING-IN-PUBLICATION DATA

Davidson, MaryJanice.
    Undead and unworthy / by MaryJanice Davidson.
      p. cm.
    "Wheeler Publishing Large Print Softcover"—T.p. verso.
    ISBN-13: 978-1-59722-863-3 (softcover : alk. paper)
    ISBN-10: 1-59722-863-X (softcover : alk. paper)
    1. Taylor, Betsy (Fictitious character)—Fiction. 2. Sinclair, Eric
(Fictitious character)—Fiction. 3. Newlyweds—Fiction.
    4. Vampires—Fiction. 5. Large type books. I. Title.
    PS3604.A949U5285 2008b
    813'.6—dc22   2008035519

Published in 2008 by arrangement with The Berkley Publishing Group,
a member of Penguin Group (USA) Inc.

Printed in the United States of America
1 2 3 4 5 6 7 12 11 10 09 08

For my dear husband,
who remains undaunted.

ACKNOWLEDGMENTS

How about that dedication, huh? (I know, I know. It's so gauche to pat yourself on the back . . . and in the section where you're supposed to be thanking other people!)

It's like that old saying, "May you live in interesting times," which sounds nice if you don't sit down and think 'er over, but which is really kind of horrifying.

And I'm not leading up to anything here. That dedication wasn't a dig at my husband, who's only the funniest, smartest, and coolest guy in the — in the — ever. Okay? Ever. I know people twice his age who are half as smart.

Hmm. That was more flattering when we were twenty.

Well, bottom line, he's awesome, and I'm lucky, but I had to use that dedication, because it made me think "that was just like that dedication about interesting times," and I always wished I could think up a

7

vague dedication, something a little more interesting than "To Spot, the greatest Dalmatian ever!!!!!!" and then I did, and so there you go.

And I know what you're thinking: "I didn't shoplift this MJD book for mush, for schmaltz, for a bunch of ooooh-I-love-him-so-much crapola. I shoplifted it for sarcasm and a lightweight plot!" And you'll have that, I promise. It's just that I don't always give credit where credit is due, is all. And I wanted to be sure to do that this time.

Which brings me to other family members. As always, they are relentlessly funny and knee-weakeningly supportive. As always, I don't usually notice at the time, but end up absurdly grateful after the fact.

Thanks to my children, who make being a full-time writer easy, because they're so darned low maintenance. Just last month I walked in on my mother showing my youngest where I'd dedicated a book to him, and it was a beautiful scene. "See? That's about you. That's you, honey, on a page with a first American print run of six figures, which will of course be increased at no hesitation if there is sufficient public demand, so give this to your teacher and talk it up at show and tell, all right?"

And my son was all, "That's nice, I'd like

a pear now."

Well, okay, not really. I mean, his reaction was real. Pretty much verbatim. That stuff my mom said was made up after the second "you." Although she is very supportive. Hand-sells lots of my books. You know that strange woman who walks right up to you and starts chatting about her stupid kid, who you've never met and never want to meet, but who apparently writes (yawn), and you buy her kid's dumb book so you don't hurt her feelings, because, even if she's lightly medicated, she's really nice? That's my mom.

And the tall guy lurking in the background ready to defend her honor — seriously, he will *kick* your *ass* if you look at her sideways. He's as quick to get down and rumble now as he was in his twenties. In his own disturbing way, also supportive.

The other child they had, who will correct booksellers if she spots my books spine-side out in stacks, instead of cover side out? My sister. (Booksellers, beware.)

There's a bunch of other nutwads in the family tree who deserve mentioning, I mean, we haven't even *touched* on the in-laws yet, and that's a whole other family tree of monkeys. But I'm starting to get bored, and if I am, you've gotta be snoring.

9

Or close to it.

Anyway, thanks, everybody. For everything.

AUTHOR'S NOTE

This book takes place two months after the events of *Undead and Uneasy* and *Dead Over Heels*. Also cops, like pharmacists, are weird. They can't help it. It's a hazard of their occupation. It's also why they're cool.

Finally, my father was a valuable resource for this book; he's an encyclopedia of guns and ammo. Any mistakes are mine, not his.

A NOTE TO THE READER

This book, book seven of the Undead series (book *seven!* Jesus!), is the beginning of a new story arc. You probably noticed a change in the cover design (if you're reading the American version, that is), among other things, and that is indicative of the new direction I'm taking the series in.

Just as the first six books in the series were their own story arc, so the next three books will be an arc . . . think of this book as the first of a trilogy within a series.

My point being, if you get to the end, you needn't fear . . . there's more to come. Unless you're not a Betsy fan, in which case . . . be afraid. Be very afraid.

— MaryJanice Davidson
Minneapolis, MN
Winter 2008

The Queene hath dominion over all the dead, and they shalt take from her, as she takes from them, and she shalt noe them, and they her, for that is what it is to be Queene.

and

The Queene shalt see oceans of blood, and despair.
— THE BOOK OF THE DEAD

Frivolous: Unworthy of serious attention; trivial: *a frivolous novel.*
— THE AMERICAN HERITAGE DICTIONARY OF THE ENGLISH LANGUAGE, FOURTH EDITION

I would rather go to any extreme than suffer anything that is **unworthy** of my reputation, or of that of my crown.
— ELIZABETH I (1533–1603)

Out of me **unworthy** and unknown
The vibrations of deathless music.
— "ANNE RUTLEDGE,"
BY EDGAR LEE MASTERS (1869–1950)

CHAPTER 1

Bored, I crossed the carpet in five steps, climbed up on Sinclair's desk, and kissed him. My left knee dislodged the phone, which hit the floor with a muffled thump and instantly started making that annoying *eee-eee-eee* sound. My right skidded on a fax Sinclair had gotten from some bank.

Surprised, but always up for a nooner (or whatever vampires called sex at 7:30 at night), my husband kissed me back with enthusiasm. Meanwhile, due to the afore-mentioned knee-skidding, I slammed into him so hard, his chair hit the wall with enough force to put a crack in the wallpaper. More work for the handyman.

He yanked, and my (cashmere! argh) sweater tore down the middle. He shoved, and my skirt (Ann Taylor) went up. He pulled, and my panties (Target) went who knew where? And I was pretty busy tugging and pulling at his suit (try as I might, I could not get the king of the vampires to *not* wear a suit), so the cloth was flying.

He did that sweep-the-top-of-the-desk thing you see in movies and plopped me on my back. He reached down, and I said, "Not the shoes!" so he left them alone (although I noticed the eye roll and made a mental note to bitch about it later).

He tugged, pulled, and entered. It hurt a little, because normally I needed more than sixteen seconds of foreplay, but it was also pretty fucking great (literally!).

I wrapped my legs around his waist, so I could admire my sequined leopard-print pumps (don't even ask me what they cost). Then I grinned up at him, I couldn't help it, and he smiled back, his dark eyes narrow with lust. It was so awesome to be a newlywed. And I was almost done with my thank-you notes!

I let my head fall back, enjoying the feel of him, the smell of him, his hands on my waist, his dick filling me up, his mouth on my neck, kissing, licking, then biting.

Then my dead stepmother said, "This is all your fault, Betsy, and I'm not going anywhere until you fix it."

To which I replied, "Aaaaah! Aaaaah! AAAAAAHHHHHHH!"

Sinclair jerked like I'd turned into sunshine and spoke for the first time since I swept into his office. "Elizabeth, what's wrong? Am I hurting you?"

"Aaaaaaaaaaaahhhhhhhhhh!"

From my vantage point, my dead step-mother was upside down, which somehow made it all the more terrible, because, contrary to popular belief, you *can't* turn a frown upside down.

"You can fuss all you want, but you've got responsibilities, and don't think I don't know it." She shook her head at me, and in death, as in life, her overly coiffed pineapple-blond hair didn't move. She was wearing a fuchsia skirt, a low-cut sky blue blouse, black nylons, and fuchsia pumps. Also, too much makeup. It practically hurt to look at her. "So you better get to work."

"Aaaaaaaaaaahhhhhhhhhh!"

Sinclair pulled out and started frantically feeling me. "Where are you hurt?"

"The Ant! The Ant!"

"You — what?"

Before I could elaborate (and where to begin?), I heard thundering footsteps, and then Marc slammed into the closed office door. His scent was unmistakeable — anti-septic and dried blood.

I heard him back off and grab for the doorknob, and then he was standing in the doorway. "Betsy, are you — oh my God!" He went red so fast I was afraid he was going to have a stroke. "I'm sorry, jeez, I thought that was a bad 'aaaaahhhh,' not a sex 'aaaaahhh.' "

More footsteps, and then my best friend, Jessica, was saying, "What's wrong? Is she okay?" She was so skinny and short, I couldn't see her behind Marc.

"The Ant is here!" I yowled, as Sinclair assembled the rags of his suit, picked me up off the desk, and shoved me behind him. I don't know why he bothered; Marc was gay *and* a doctor, and so couldn't care less if I was mostly naked. And Jessica had seen me naked about a million times. "Here, right now!"

"Your stepmother's in this room?" I still couldn't see her, but Jessica's tone managed to convey the sheer horror I felt at the prospect of being haunted by the Ant.

"Where *else* would I be?" the Ant, the late Antonia Taylor, said reasonably. She was tapping her Payless-clad foot and nibbling her lower lip. "What I'd like to know is, where's your father?"

"Yeah, that's all this scene is missing," I fumed. "If only my dead dad were here, too."

CHAPTER 2

After Marc decided a Valium drip probably wouldn't work on a vampire, he brought me a stiff drink instead. Could he even tap a vein? I was over a year dead, after all. Would an IV take? Someday I was going to have to sit down and figure all this shit out. Someday when I wasn't plagued by ghosts, serial killers, wedding planning, rogue werewolves, mysterious vampires bursting in on me, and diaper changing.

It was sweet of Marc to bring me a gin and tonic (which I loathed, but he didn't know that), but I was so rattled I drank it off in one gulp, and it could have been paint thinner, for all I knew.

"Is she still here?" he whispered.

"Of course I'm still here," my dead stepmother snapped. "I told you, I'm not going anywhere."

"I'm the only one who can hear you," I shrilled, "so just shut up!"

"Bring her another drink," Sinclair muttered. We were still in his office, but Jessica had kindly brought robes to cover our shredded clothes. "Bring her three."

"I don't need booze, I need to get rid of you know what."

"Very funny," the Ant grumped.

She and my father had been killed in a gruesome, stupid car accident a couple of months ago. Where she had been since her death, and why she had shown up now, I didn't know. There were so many things about being the vampire queen I didn't know! And I didn't *want* to know.

But I was going to have to find out, because the ghosts never, ever went away, until I solved their little problems for them.

And where *was* my dead dad, anyway? I sighed. Nonconfrontational in life as well as in death.

"What do you want?"

"I *told* you. To fix this."

"Fix *what?*"

"*You* know."

"This is so weird," Marc murmured to Jessica, forgetting, as usual, about superior vamp hearing. "She's having a conversation with the chair."

"She is not. Quiet so I can hear."

"I *don't* know," I said to the chair —- uh,

the Ant. "I really, really don't. Please tell me."

"Stop playing games."

"I'm *not!*" I almost screamed. Then I felt Sinclair's soothing hands on my shoulders and sagged into him. Like our honeymoon hadn't been stressful enough, what with all the dead kids and Jessica and her boyfriend crashing it and all. This was a hundred times worse.

"If you could just —" I began, when the office door crashed open, nearly smashing into Marc, who yelped and jumped aside.

A bloody, stinking horror was framed in the doorway, then darted right at me like a goblin in a fairy tale. Since I was a tad keyed up from the Ant popping in, my reflexes were in excellent shape. I slugged the thing — it was a man, a big, bearish, shambling man — so hard I knocked him halfway across the office. He hit the carpet so hard, buttons popped off his shirt, which looked about ready for the ragbag anyway.

He was on his feet in a flash and looked wildly from Sinclair to me and back again. And he was — there was something familiar about him. Something I couldn't put my finger on.

Sinclair and I started toward him in unison, and he backed up, pivoted, and

23

dived out the second story window.

"What the blue hell — ?" I began.

The office door crashed open, and I felt like clutching my heart. I couldn't stand many more of these shocks to my system.

Garrett, the Fiend formerly known as George, stood in the doorway, panting. Since he was seventy-some years old and didn't need to breathe, I knew at once something was seriously wrong.

What fresh hell was this?

"They're awake," he gasped. "And they want to kill you."

"Who?" Sinclair, Jessica, Marc, and I asked in unison. It could be anyone. The guys who delivered pizza from Green Mill. Other vampires. The Ant's book club. Werewolves. Zombies. And, of course, the uninvited guest who'd jumped out the window. So many enemies, so little —

"The other Fiends. I've been feeding them my blood, and they're pissed."

"You've what, and they're what?" I asked, horrified.

Garrett couldn't look at me — never a good sign. "They — they sort of 'woke up,' and now they want to kill you."

"It's this lifestyle you lead," the Ant said smugly. "These things are bound to happen."

24

"Oh, shut up!" I barked. I actually had to clutch my head; which problem to tackle first? "You couldn't have crashed into the office tomorrow? Or yesterday?"

"You'd better sit down and tell us every-thing," Sinclair said, reminding me he was the vampire king. "The queen has just been attacked . . . and now you come bearing tales of murder." Bam. Decision made. We'd deal with what Garrett had done first.

So take that, dead stepmother.

CHAPTER 3

Like I wasn't dreading the coming winter already. These days I was always cold, even on the hottest day in July; November was going to suck rocks. What I wanted to do was adjust to married life, set up house (well, the house had been set up for more than a year, thanks to Jessica and her big bucks, but I was still finding places for our wedding gifts), finish writing thank-you notes (yawn), and settle down to the job of raising BabyJon, my half brother and legal ward. (You remember, the whole my dad and the Ant being dead thing.)

Yep, yep. Everything was normal. I was a newlywed and would-be parent. Nothing wrong or weird here. Nope.

"— felt responsible," Garrett was yakking, which in itself was hard to get used to. He'd gone from slobbering Fiend to monosyllabic boyfriend (Antonia-the-werewolf's stud . . . more on that later) to verbose old vampire.

The fact that he *looked* about twenty-three didn't fool anybody. "So I began visiting them. It didn't seem right that I was back to myself while they were — were — well. You know."

Fine time for his newfound vocabulary to fail him! But we knew. The old king — the one I'd killed to take the crown — liked to torture newly risen vampires by refusing to let them feed. After a few months of this treatment, they went crazy. Worse than crazy — feral. Forgot everything they ever knew, or could know, about being human. Think dangerous, rabid wolves, wearing L.L. Bean.

Sinclair and his major domo, Tina, had asked me again and again to stake the Fiends through the heart.

But I couldn't. It'd be like stomping puppies. Blood-thirsty, feral, dangerous puppies, yes, but still — puppies. Had I made the puppies? No. Was any of it the puppies' fault? Nope. Was I going to kill — worse yet, order to kill, wouldn't even have to get my hands dirty — innocent puppies, no matter how many buckets of blood they drank a day?

No.

And now the puppies were going to eat out my soft human heart. You'd think I'd have learned the essential Rule of the Undead by now: cuddly undead are still undead.

"How come nobody tried feeding them their own blood before?" Marc asked. "Why the buckets of animal blood?"

"They're too dangerous to be allowed to hunt. They'll kill anyone they can find."

"Yeesh."

"I don't think we have time for a recap," Garrett said, nervously cocking his head to one side. "Recap," that was very good; man, he was sharp! Picking up slang like no tomorrow. To think, six months ago he couldn't even purl, much less knit.

"But Garrett fed them his blood. 'Live' blood — so to speak. So, how come nobody tried that before?"

"Nobody," Sinclair said, the corners of his mouth drawing down, "cares to get near them. No offense, Garrett."

"None taken, my king," he said stiffly, not looking at my husband.

And there it was. The Fiends were the untouchables, the unwashed. In a society built of nonhumans, of monsters, these guys were considered a level below that. A good trick, if you sat down and thought it over.

I smacked my forehead with the palm of my hand. "I *knew* I recognized that guy!

He's one of the Fiends? Jesus, he's really out?"

"Did somebody break a window?" Tina asked, walking into the office with what appeared to be a ream of paperwork waiting for Sinclair's signature. Privately, my husband was the king of the vampires; publicly, he owned several companies, tracts of land, and office buildings and was ridiculously wealthy. Half mine now, under Minnesota law. I think. Or — wait. Were we a community property state or — I guess I'd blocked out most of my mom and dad's divorce —

"Garrett brought the Fiends back to life like some kind of moody 1920s Frankenstein, and now they're on their way here to kill Betsy," Marc said in one breath, looking pleased at his ability to spit out several words without passing out. Of all the nights for him not to be on call at the ER! There'd be no shaking him off our heels tonight. Normally, we tried to keep the respirating roommates out of vampire biz, for their own safety if nothing else.

"They're what? Who's here to *what?*" Tina's jaw sagged; papers fluttered. She was a doll of a woman with waist-length blond hair and enormous pansy eyes. She looked delicious in knee-length shirtdresses and nonprescription glasses she didn't need. She was wearing both, in navy and tortoiseshell. "Why are you all standing around? Why —"

"Also, the Ant has started haunting me."

"I was wondering when you'd remember I existed," the wretched woman snapped.

"Did you remember to pick up tampons?" Jessica asked, and now the *men* looked appalled. That was a good question, actually. I sure didn't need them anymore, ergo Tina didn't. Jessica's cycle had been all over the place since the cancer. Did Antonia — any female werewolf, for that matter — need them? The ghost definitely didn't.

And what did it say about my life that I was living (again) with two women named Antonia? Most people went their entire lives without running into an Antonia. When one of them died, I figured I was home freaking free! Really, it was all —

"Majesty, will you focus!"

"Huh? Why?"

Sinclair actually laughed out loud while Tina stomped a tiny foot. "Angry vampires are on their way here to kill you."

"It's hard to get worked up," I said truthfully as my husband bit back another laugh, "when the Ant is breathing over my shoulder. So to speak. And it's not exactly the first time unwelcome guests have been on

30

the way." I turned to Jessica. "Remember homecoming 1996?"

She shuddered. "I never thought you'd get the Dewar's out of the curtains."

"But I guess we'll just have to —"

Bam! Ka-Bam! BAM! BAM! BAM!

"*What* the — ?" Jessica wondered.

"That would be hordes of the ravenous undead, kicking in the front door," Tina said, dropping the rest of the paperwork and whipping off her glasses. I waited for her to do a Wonder Woman twirl (Wonder Vamp!), but she just looked alert and ready to flee.

Sinclair sighed, looking greatly put upon. But men who have interrupted sex tend to get that look. "Shall we flee, or fight?"

Tina glanced at Jessica, who glared. "Ah. Flee, I think. At least until we know more about this particular threat."

"Don't run off on my account," Jessica warned. But of course, that's exactly why we were choosing flight over fight. We couldn't risk Marc and Jessica's lives until we knew more about what was going on. "I mean it, you guys."

Sinclair ignored her. "Very well. Let's take the tunnel."

Tunnel? We were taking a tunnel? We had the king, the queen, Tina, a former Fiend — the odds were okay, I thought. But Tina

31

had an excellent point — we had a couple of humans to watch out for, too.

Tina led the way to one of the many doors leading to the basement, and I had to jog to keep up. "What? We have a tunnel?"

"Betsy, come *on!*" Marc said, grabbing an elbow and giving such a yank I nearly fell down the stairs.

"Not without me, you're not," the Ant said triumphantly, and marched (Marched? Couldn't she float?) behind me just as the door closed, leaving all of us in pure darkness.

CHAPTER 4

Well. Not *pure.* I could see fine, as could Garrett, Tina, and Sinclair. But from the moans and whimpers coming from farther down the stairs, the humans were having more trouble.

"Stop that sniveling, Marc Spangler, or I'll de-testicle you," Jessica snapped. When she was scared, she got pissed. Man, you should have seen her the day she got a false positive on an EPT. We were buying new dishes for days.

"I can't see a fucking thing," he snarled back. There was an abrupt silence, a — I know how this sounds, but I could hear it — a flailing, and then a rattle of thumps, followed by moans of pain.

"Getting eaten alive by the Fiends can't be worse than this," Marc groaned from the floor. Ouch. He must have fallen at least ten steps. Onto cement.

"Be careful," Tina said.

"Thanks. At least someone cares."

"You could have broken your ankle on the way down and slowed our escape."

"I hate vampires," he replied. "So much."

I eased past Jessica on the stairs, went to Marc, and picked him up. "This is so romantic," he cooed, modestly kicking his unbroken foot.

"Shut up, or I'll use you for Fiend chum."

"Why," Jessica demanded, "have we decamped to the basement?"

"And why haven't we turned any lights on?" I asked.

"Tina, take Jessica's hand. Elizabeth, keep carrying Marc." Sinclair groaned softly in the dark, as if he couldn't believe he'd said such a thing. "Everyone else, follow me."

It took a long time. The basement was as long as the house, which was a mansion on Summit Avenue. And we had to wander around various tables and chairs, in and out of mysterious rooms — I could count on one hand how often I'd been down here since we moved a couple of years ago. I had never liked it, not even — especially even — when Garrett was living down there, knitting afghans and learning to crochet.

The journey wasn't improved by the occasional yelps, as Jessica stubbed a toe or cracked an elbow. Marc just snuggled

34

deeper into my arms (ridiculous — he had thirty pounds of muscle on me) and waited patiently for me to make him safe.

Story of my life, since I'd died.

CHAPTER 5

We could hear faint crashings from upstairs; the Fiends, making a mess because they couldn't find us. Chewing on my drapes; defecating on my carpet, ripping up my graphic novels in their bloodthirsty rage. But surely they could follow their noses?

That's when Sinclair stopped walking and began tapping his knuckles on what looked like a solid cement wall.

"I don't think you should do that," I said nervously. "They might hear."

"Over the sound of their own nonsense? Doubtful."

I opened my mouth to object again (quietly) when the solid cement wall suddenly swung wide to the left, revealing a narrow, dimly lit (with fluorescents, blinking on one by one even as we stared) tunnel.

"Tunnel?" I asked, peering.

"Tunnel," Marc confirmed, peering with

me. His grip tightened around my neck. "Did this come with the house, or did you put it in after?"

Good fucking question, which, I couldn't help notice, my husband didn't bother to answer.

"The lights and heat are motion activated." Sinclair turned to me, smiling with all his sharp teeth. "Usually, in our case, heat activation would do little good. After you, my queen."

Wondering what else about the Vampiric Mansion of Mystery I didn't know, I went.

CHAPTER 6

"I'm tired," I whined after we'd been walking for a hundred years.

"It's only a bit farther," my lying bastard husband said.

"You keep *saying* that, and we keep not *being* there."

"I keep *dreaming* about divorce and not *being* divorced."

"Oh, very nice!" I raged, running to catch up with them, ignoring Marc's yelps as he was jolted in my arms. "Married not even a season, and you're looking for the door, *such* a typical guy, I knew you — hey!"

I had been lifted easily, effortlessly. "Now shush, Your Majesty," Tina said, shifting my and Marc's combined weight with no effort. "And we really are almost there."

"This," Marc announced over the distinctive gagging noise of Jessica stifling laughter, "is too much. My masculinity could stand being carried by Betsy, but —"

"The gay guy has concerns about masculinity?" Jessica managed, then broke down completely.

"I'm gay, not a eunuch. Have you ever seen me in drag? Or even mascara? I'm a regular guy in every way —"

"Except you like to put your penis in weird places," I said primly.

"Can we please have one midnight getaway without having to talk about Marc's penis?" Tina asked, aggrieved.

We all shut up as we navigated another set of stairs . . . and then another. I'd been living here for months and months, and *nobody had told me about the secret vampire escape tunnel.*

I remembered that Sinclair had steered Jessica toward this house when we had to upgrade. Back in the days when I thought I hated him. And here I thought it had been because he was a history buff and liked old houses!

"I've never been bored, and scared, at the same time," Marc commented.

"What do you want me to do with that information?" Tina asked.

"Just put us down," he grumbled, and Tina did, hard enough to rattle my teeth. Marc and I groaned in unison.

Sinclair pressed another button, another

wall raised, and I suddenly could hear flowing water. He walked out into what must have looked like pure darkness to the others, except I could hear his heels clanking on the boards of the dock. He sounded like a sheriff from the Old West.

"We walked all the way to the Mississippi?" Marc goggled.

"What 'we'?" Jessica asked. "And it was, what? Seven, eight whole blocks?"

We heard Sinclair start up the Evinrude, and as he hit the lights Jessica and Marc cheered.

"Get the rope, will you, darling?" he asked casually, as if he didn't look, at that moment, like the coolest guy in the universe.

The dock was a memory a few seconds later, and when Sinclair opened 'er up, I decided I wasn't mad anymore and allowed him to put his arm around me.

CHAPTER 7

"All right, Garrett," my husband said about half an hour later. I had no idea where we were, but we were out of the Fiends' reach, at least for now. He'd powered down the motor, and we were floating between a couple of islands. City lights were visible, but far off. I'd always sucked at geography; the lights could have been St. Paul or Minneapolis for all I knew. "Suppose you tell us everything."

I realized that during our tunnel getaway and subsequent penis discussion, Garrett hadn't said word one. And at some point, the Ant had disappeared. Thank goodness for small etcetera.

Garrett, a slim, tall blond with hair almost as long as Marc's, was sitting low in the bow, staring at his hands.

"Garrett? Helloooo? Time, if you didn't notice by the whole Fiends breaking down the door and the tunnel escape, is not on

41

our side."

"I am shamed," he said at last, still staring at his hands. "I feel ashamed."

"Well," Marc said reasonably, swiveling around in one of the captain's chairs, "what'd you do?"

He looked up at me, the moonlight bouncing off his face and making his eyes seem to gleam. "You should kill me, dread queen. Right now."

"Blech! I mean, uh, no way, Garrett, you're one of the family." The giant extended family I neither wanted nor asked for. To think, three years ago I was living in a two-bedroom in Apple Valley, bitching because I hadn't had a date in over a month. My biggest problem had been fixing the copy machine at my day job — management *would* try to fuck with the machines, and often there was no hope afterward. "Besides, if I didn't kill you when you were a Fiend, I'm sure not going to now and risk your girlfriend's wrath." Antonia-the-werewolf was a high octane bitch when she was in a *good* mood. I never, never wanted to see her when she was really mad.

"Antonia," Garrett said, almost sighed. "As you know, my mate has to leave me. Often, she leaves. More so, now that you changed her."

We nodded, like we'd been cued. We did know this. Antonia had to pop over to Cape Cod now and again — the seat of werewolf power, pardon me while I snigger — and tend to pack business. We assumed she didn't take Garrett, because traveling with a vampire could get tricky.

Also, up until two months ago, she was a werewolf who had never changed during the full moon. I had done something to her, something we all still didn't like to talk about, and now she *did* change. The meetings on Cape Cod had increased as a result, but those of us in the manse weren't talking about it.

"I stay," he continued, "because I'm afraid."

"Of what?" Jessica asked.

"The world," he replied simply. "The last time I went out in the world, I was captured and bound like a slave."

Thank you, Marjorie, you kidnapping fuck, may you roast in Hell for a zillion billion years.

"The time before that, I was killed. The monster got me. I don't go out in the world anymore."

It occurred to me (it was going to be a night of discovering things that had been under my nose) that except for going after

43

Antonia last summer (and getting captured, as he put it, and bound like a slave), I couldn't remember the last time he had left the mansion.

I imagined he fed on Antonia, but such things were none of my business, so I didn't ask. As long as he wasn't hurting innocent people, I had no interest in where he was getting his liquid diet.

"An agoraphobic vampire?" Marc asked, and I could tell he was trying very, very hard not to laugh.

"It's more common than you might think," Tina said, pacing the small deck. She was so light on her feet, the boat didn't even rock. "Particularly when the vampire in question had a bad death."

"Uh, excuse me, but don't you guys have to kill somebody for them to come back? Aren't all vampires, by definition, murder victims? They all sound like bad deaths to me."

"Point," Jessica said, actually sticking her left index finger in the air to mark the point.

"So, didn't you guys all have bad deaths? Except for Betsy?"

"Call me the day after *you* get run over by an Aztec, and then we'll talk," I grumbled.

"We are not here to discuss such things with — with guests," Sinclair said, correcting himself so smoothly Tina and I were probably the only ones who knew he'd been about to say "outsiders" or "humans." "And you were telling us about Antonia."

"Other than my mate, I have no peers. All of you, even the humans, are smarter than I."

"What 'even'?" Marc said. "I'm a doctor."

Jessica put a soothing hand on Marc's arm. "Garrett, don't be so hard on yourself. You've been out of it for, what? Sixty, seventy years? Crack a few modern history books, you'll be up to speed in no time."

Garrett waited patiently until Jessica was finished. "It is not my place to befriend a queen, or a king. So when Antonia leaves me, I am lonely."

I was beginning to see where this was going. Oh, it'd be a lovely children's book: *Garrett the Fiend Finds Friends!*

"And it seemed to me that I was — that I was the way I am now — because the good queen and the devil's daughter allowed me to feed off them. I thought perhaps if I gave my old comrades my blood . . ."

Okay. This is a little embarrassing to explain, so I'm just gonna plunge in and get it over with. See, I *had* let Garrett feed from me, ages ago. And as a sort of punishment, I'd ordered the devil's daughter to do the

45

same thing.

The devil's daughter being my half sister, Laura.

(I know. Bear with me.)

See, the Ant was possessed by the devil years back, only she was so fucking nasty nobody noticed. And the devil didn't care for child rearing, so she dumped Laura and took off back to Hell. Laura was adopted by (seriously, don't laugh) a minister and his wife.

How do you rebel against the evilest nastiest yuckiest entity in the universe (who looks like Lena Olin and has an amazing shoe collection)?

You go to church. You teach Sunday school. You don't touch a drop of booze until your twenty-first birthday.

And you conceal a hateful, murderous temper. Laura was going to blow one of these days, but I just didn't have time to worry about it right now. Among other things, I had slavering Fiends on my tail and thank-you cards to finish.

"So I began to visit them and let them feed off me."

"Eh?"

"Pay attention, Elizabeth."

"They didn't try to puree you or anything?" Marc asked.

Garrett shook his head. "Even though I had . . . changed, they still knew me as one of them. They would never have hurt me. Or so I thought, until tonight. And I felt . . . bad. To see them. I had everything, and they were drinking buckets of cow blood."

I was suddenly interested in studying my feet. I wouldn't have credited Garrett with a guilty conscience. But then, I scarcely thought about him at all.

"I was not sure what would happen, but I kept trying. I had found so much happiness in —"

"Your agoraphobia," Marc prompted.

"— in my new life, I felt it cost me nothing but blood to try to help my old friends. And Antonia is generous with her blood. She regenerates quickly, as is part of her superior genetic heritage."

"Superior genetic —" Tina began, equal parts outraged and interested (until a very short time ago, neither she nor Sinclair believed in werewolves), but Sinclair shook his head, and she shut up without another word. God, I'd love to learn that trick. I'd only use it for fighting evil, though.

"It worked. My friends were helped by my blood. The effect wasn't all at once. It took many visits. It was — was —"

"Accumulative?" Jessica and Marc asked

47

in unison.

Garrett nodded.

"But they weren't really friends, right?" I asked anxiously. "You guys didn't even know each other in life, right? Once in a while, ole Nostril would take it in his teeny brain and toss another one of you into the snake pit and that was about it. Right?"

"We were prisoners together," Garrett said quietly, "for decades."

"Right, right, got that, sorry." I was so embarrassed I couldn't look at him. So I went back to studying my toes. "So, you had good intentions, right?"

"Exactly so, my queen," he said eagerly. "I only wished —"

"And in your loneliness and self-exile, you put the queen's life in danger," Sinclair said coldly. "You put her friends in danger, and my friend." I noticed he didn't include himself in the pack. "I should have ignored Elizabeth's soft heart and staked you myself."

I heard Tina flip open the seat on the stern (you could sit on it, but it held life jackets and things . . . sort of like a padded cedar chest), rummage around, and produce — ack! — a stake. The boat that had everything!

Garrett sank to his knees. "All you say is

true, bold king," he said to the deck.

"Marc, Jessica, step to the back. You don't want to get splashed."

"Now wait just a fucking minute!" I slapped the stake out of Tina's hand so hard she nearly plunged overboard. (And what other nasty implements of death were in that chest?)

I marched over and hauled Garrett to his feet. The book rocked alarmingly, then steadied. "This is a monarchy, right, Sinclair? And if the Book of the Dead is right, *I* outrank *you*. I was *born* the queen; you had to fuck me to get your crown."

And oh, boy, I still got pissed if I thought that one over too carefully.

"So I'll be the one to say who gets staked." I shook Garrett, who drooped at the end of my arm. "Stand up straight! Defend yourself! Be a man of the early twentieth century, for God's sake — ignorant yet sure of your superiority." (We were sure he'd been killed in the thirties or forties.)

"Ever the graceful hostess," Sinclair commented.

"Besides, smart guy, you didn't even notice that every time Antonia left town, Garrett was leaving the house and feeding other vampires. Too busy looking for new companies to buy?"

"Touché," Tina muttered, not looking happy about it. Watching over the estate, including the Fiend farm, was part of her job, but she knew I preferred to yell at Sinclair rather than her.

"So, Garrett, where were we? What's the rest of the story?"

"My plan worked," he continued miserably. "Too well, I fear . . . my comrades wanted to know where they were, what had happened to them. Unlike me, they were — were displeased to find themselves —"

"Stuck on an abandoned farm full of animal blood?" Jessica suggested.

"Exactly so. I tried to emphasize the queen's goodness in letting them live, tried to explain that she had set us free by killing our jailor, but they only became more enraged. Essentially, they could not understand —"

"Why you and not them?" Marc asked.

"What?" I cried. "So this is *my* fault?"

"Looks like," Jessica replied.

"They were so angry," Garrett said dolefully.

"Angry? After you saved them? Ungrateful brutes. Besides, with Nostro dead, what's to be mad about?" Marc asked.

"Ah, let me count the ways," Sinclair purred. And he did just that, ticking the points off on his long, slender fingers. "They are angry because they are old vampires with no real power. Deprived of live blood for so long, like Garrett, they will never have real power. They are angry about, as they see it, being dumped on a farm, and never mind that it was for the public's safety."

"But it was!" I cried.

"The vampire queen puts vampires first, my dearest. As I have repeatedly told you. Next —"

"I don't wanna hear any more," I groaned.

"— they are angry that a new queen has been in power for two years and done nothing to help them —"

"Nothing! I stopped you from killing them about nine times!"

"— angry that the new queen knows she could have 'cured' them at any time (case in point, the happily married, articulate Garrett), and, finally, extremely angry that they've been given silly nicknames."

"That wasn't the queen," Tina said loyally. "That was Alice."

"Alice is dead," Garrett said.

"Happy, Skippy, Trippy, Sandy, Benny, Clara, and Jane killed her?" I said, horrified.

"I tried to stop them, but they are many, and I am one. I only barely escaped myself.

Alice . . ." He looked away, out over the water. "Died cursing me."

"And then you led them straight to the queen."

Garrett shivered. "I had not — thought of that. My only thought was to return to safety. One of them followed me. He must have picked up the queen's scent — from my clothes, I think — and —"

"Blown past you, beat you to the mansion. You fell for the oldest trick in the book," Marc said, not unkindly. "Leading the bad guys to the good guys."

"I am a coward. I was afraid to be alone, and now I have endangered you all."

"Well, now, uh, that's a little harder to defend," I admitted, "but you didn't set out to do bad."

Sinclair made a disgusted sound and threw his hands up in the air. "Elizabeth, really!"

"If I went around killing everyone who made a mistake, I'd be pretty damned lonely," I snapped back. I actually patted the trembling Garrett. "Nobody's going to kill you, Garrett."

"Well, maybe some of his old friends," Jessica said helpfully.

"Yeah," I sighed. "There's that. Ideas?"

CHAPTER 8

We (Sinclair) decided to go to the farm to
check out the scene of the crime. We
(Sinclair) figured it was best to see if things
were as bad as Garrett intimated. And no
one was in a rush to get back to the mansion.

Nostro had, once upon a time, owned this
property, and I had been, once upon a time,
a prisoner here. And getting here had taken
no time at all . . . once Tina's cell got a
signal, she made a call, Sinclair docked the
boat at some teeny marina, and an empty,
idling SUV was waiting for us.

"It's good to be the king," Marc murmured in my ear, as we all climbed in, making me giggle.

Under no circumstances would Jessica
and Marc allow themselves to be dumped
somewhere safe. The argument got so
heated that Sinclair pulled over on a quiet
corner of Minnetonka (at this hour, every

corner in Minnetonka was quiet) so we could disembark onto the sidewalk and discuss (read: shriek) it without endangering nearby traffic.

It was only when I saw Sinclair gliding behind Jessica when I realized (a) she couldn't hear him, and (b) what his plan was.

"Don't you *dare* knock her unconscious!"

"I wasn't going to!" Marc yelled back, flinching away from me.

"Or him, either," I added, noticing Tina sidling up to Marc.

"It would have been for their own safety," El Sneako grumbled.

"We're perfectly safe," Marc said, but then, he would. He loved all things vampire. Given that he'd been about to hurl himself from a tall building to escape his boring life when I met him, I couldn't entirely blame him. "We've got the king and queen of the vampires with us and, a, um, shell of a vampire to bring up the rear."

For Garrett had been no good at all since we got off the boat. He shivered, he shook, he tried to curl up. It was obvious that, since we weren't going to kill him, being outside made him miserable. For the first time I noticed how torn his clothing was, though his injuries had healed. Old, Sinclair had said, and that was certainly true. But not powerful. Never powerful. There had been a time after I brought him home like a stray when we thought . . . but no.

Old, but not powerful. Poor guy.

As we grumpily climbed back into the SUV, I wondered again about power. What, exactly, made a vampire powerful? Not age, certainly (I was two!), or at least, not *just* age. I had been told that, like me, Sinclair had risen strong. Most vampires went through a ten-year phase where they'd do anything for blood and couldn't remember their own names.

Was determination a factor? Anger, hate, vanity? Hmm, that last could explain my meteoric rise to power . . .

"We're here," Sinclair said abruptly, braking hard enough to make my seat belt lock (force of habit; no real reason to wear the thing these days). "And you two will *stay here.* I mean it, Marc. Jessica. Remain *in this vehicle,* or I will be cross."

"Excuse me, captain my captain," Marc said, "but do you know how many horror movies start out like this?"

"We probably shouldn't split up," Jessica agreed. "Besides, if you really thought the Fiends were still here, you'd never have let us come. You'd have clocked Betsy, too, if it had come to that."

Sinclair muttered something that the chime of the "door open" light drowned out; sounded like "wretched woman." We all solemnly clambered out with him, knowing that even if Marc and Jess had won a victory, it was nothing to celebrate.

CHAPTER 9

We were okay until we found Alice's body. Sure, there had been an obvious fight, the fence had been torn open in several places, there were splashes of blood on the ground, but . . . really, I was okay until we found her head.

While Marc supported Jessica as she threw up in the chokecherry bushes (he was pale, but had seen so much death as a doctor, even this couldn't make him sick) and I swayed dizzily on my feet,

(don't faint don't faint don't faint QUEENS DON'T FAINT!)

Tina and Sinclair prowled the area like vampiric bloodhounds, finding arms, legs, both halves of a torso.

"This is maybe a dumb question," Marc began, smoothing Jessica's tight black cap of curls and letting her lean on his shoulder.

(don't faint don't faint don't faint)

Tina shook her head. "There's no chance

of regeneration. Absolutely none. Frankly, I'd be amazed if the queen could handle this kind of punishment. My queen?" Her voice sharpened. "Are you all right?"

"Of course she's all right," Sinclair said, squatting to examine another body part. "Queens don't faint."

"Damn right! Look, Alice is obviously dead. What are you poking around for?"

"Oh, this and that," he said vaguely. "I'm a little puzzled by the condition of the corpse."

"I was thinking that exact thing," Tina added.

"What are you talking about?" I asked, but they were ignoring me and having their own conversation.

"Did you call —"

"Already done, my king."

"Excellent."

"Ah, and a mysterious van of vampires will show up and dispose of all the evidence," Jessica managed, wiping her mouth.

"More or less."

"I think we should go back now, can we please go back home now?"

Sinclair looked at Garrett with obvious distaste. "What makes you think it's safe?"

"I-I don't think they'd stay. Not if they couldn't find . . . her."

58

Okay, so Garrett wasn't exactly being the stand-up guy you read about in romance novels. But I felt sorry for him — it couldn't have been much fun getting the crap stomped out of him by half a dozen pissed off vampires, vampires he'd tried to *help,* and then come home to tell Sinclair what he'd done.

Sinclair didn't understand about fear, how it ate your guts, and how nobody came off like they did in the movies. He'd claimed, on occasion, to have feared for my safety, but frankly, I doubted it.

"Even if they are still there, it's our home, and a bunch of jerkoff vampires aren't keeping me out of it. I mean, you explained that to me once already, Sinclair. How we're not worthy of our crowns if our people can't find us."

"Yay, Queen Betsy," Jessica said.

"But they're sure as shit keeping you two out of it," Marc teased.

"Boo, Queen Betsy."

The argument raged all the way back home.

CHAPTER 10

Marc and Jessica's apparent casual attitude toward death was partly my fault. Make that totally. I'd saved their butts so many times (from suicide, murder, cancer) they just naturally felt impervious around me.

It didn't help that none of us were talking about it in any real detail. See, I'd always been different from other vampires. So different than even Tina (the oldest vampire I hadn't killed; she had made Sinclair way back when) didn't know much about me, or what I could do.

I had, completely by accident, cured Jessica's cancer and killed an eight-hundred-year-old vampire librarian. And I'd done it without laying a finger on the librarian. I just sort of — *pulled* her into me. What was left wouldn't have filled an urn.

That didn't bother Sinclair or Tina especially, since I'd saved Sinclair at the time. What *did* bother them was that I had no idea how I'd done it and had been unable to do so again. Not that I'd tried. *God,* no. I figured somebody would have to die for me to try out my nifty new power. Pass.

Sinclair had been spending some time in the library perusing the Book of the Dead. He thought I didn't know. But I understood his puzzlement, and I knew he was being careful.

Read that thing too long — written on human skin with blood by a centuries-dead insane vampire — and you went crazy. Upside was, it was always right. Downside, there was no index or table of contents. You just opened it and took your chances that you'd actually read something, y'know, useful.

Worst of all, it always came back to me. It had been set on fire and thrown into the Mississippi River (on two separate occasions!). It always showed up wherever I was. Fucking creepy thing that I didn't dare read and couldn't get rid of.

Or tell Sinclair I knew he was reading it. How could I bring that up without mentioning Jessica's cure, or what I did to Marjorie?

And don't even get me started on what I did to the Ant and my dad. I'd wished for a baby, and I got one — because they had been killed. It wasn't my fault, it was a

Monkey's Paw situation. I'd been wearing a cursed engagement ring at the time. One gruesome car accident later, and I was the sole guardian of my half brother, BabyJon.

Thank God he'd been spending the weekend with the devil's daughter and didn't get ripped to pieces by the Fiends!

(I can't believe I just said that. This, this is what my life had become.)

What was worse, that my distant dad and bitchy stepmother were dead, or that I didn't feel too broken up about it? Let's face it, he'd never been there for me, and she was a stiff-haired nightmare.

Who, last I checked, had been *haunting* me. Maybe I'd get lucky — maybe instead of an actual ghost, that vision of her was just a hallucination, the onset of permanent brain damage.

I sighed as we pulled into the driveway. *I should be so lucky,* I told myself.

CHAPTER 11

"This is an inopportune time," my husband pointed out as I knocked on the door at 1001 Tyler Street, a small, neatly kept gray and white house.

"No shit," I muttered. The mansion had been trashed; it was the next evening, and Jessica had called in an army of fixer-uppers. Even now, after sunset, they were still working on the house. No sign of the Fiends, and Tina had promised to get Marc and Jess into the tunnel at the first sign of trouble. She even thoughtfully provided flashlights by the entrance to the mansion basement. Even better: Marc's ankle was much better. No break, thank God.

"Then why are we here?" Sinclair asked, looking around the tidy suburban neighborhood. Inver Grove Heights was famous for their tidy suburban neighborhoods.

"Because he's been incarcerated for months, and this is the first time I've seen him since I got married."

"And . . . ?"

"I want my bigoted, angry, dying grandfather to meet my dead husband. Now slap on a smile and feel the family joy!"

Sinclair managed a friendly grimace, as the lady who ran the hospice ushered us in. It wasn't really a hospice; she was a registered nurse who owned the house, and she had three patients, including my grandpa. She could give meds and change dressings, and knew when to haul in an MD.

In return she made a reasonable living and managed not to smother my grandpa with a pillow. For their part, they were living in an actual home and not dying in an impersonal hospital ward.

"Get lost," my beloved maternal relative said warmly.

"Hi, Grandpa. Just dropped by —"

"Did you bring me a Bud?"

"— to say hi and tell you I got married."

He squinted at me with watery blue eyes. His hair was lush and entirely white — it thrived on Budweiser. His eyebrows looked like angry albino caterpillars. He was in his wheelchair by the window, dressed in sweatpants and a blue checked flannel shirt, feet sockless in the heel-less slippers.

He didn't need a wheelchair, but Mr.

Mueller in the next room had one, and my grandpa broke every plate he could find until Nurse Jenkins relented and ordered one for him. Mueller also had a colostomy bag, but my grandpa graciously decided not to go after that as well.

Next to the Ant, and maybe the devil, he was the most evil person I'd ever known. Come to think of it, most of the male influences I'd had growing up had either been —

"Your mom still fat?"

"She's at the perfect weight for her height and age, you bony smelly man!" I snapped. Great, a new record. I'd been in the same room with him for eight seconds, and already I was screaming. "It's a miracle she isn't a sociopath, raised by a rotten old man like you!"

"Hello," Sinclair said. "I'm Eric Sinclair, Elizabeth's husband."

Gramps scowled at the vampire king. "You look part Indian. You got any Injun in you, boy?"

"It's possible," Sinclair said mildly, as I moaned and chewed on a throw pillow. "I never knew my biological father."

I spit out some feathers and stared at him. "You never knew your father?"

"He could be part black!" my darling, dying relative howled. "He could be — he could be Catholic!"

"I believe I may be Californian," Sinclair added helpfully.

"*Anyway,* I got married, this is the guy, nice to see you again, don't drop dead anytime soon, because I couldn't handle another funeral this year, good-bye."

"Yup," Grandpa said, smacking his teeth (he still had them all . . . a chronic drinker and smoker with gorgeous hair and perfect teeth). "Hope that witch is having a good time screwing the devil in Hell."

"I don't think the devil swings that way," I said truthfully. I had finally remembered the one reason I hadn't wrung the old buzzard's neck twenty years ago.

Sinclair cleared his throat. I prayed he wasn't eyeing my grandpa and trying to figure out which one of the two of them was older. "Oh, you knew the, ah, late Mrs. Taylor?"

"Knew her? Beat the shit out of her."

"How sweet."

"Twat stole my girl's husband." A cat wandered near, and Grandpa kicked it away, sending his slipper flying. Sinclair snatched it out of the air and courteously handed it back. "She had to go down."

"Go . . . down?"

"Fistfight. The Halloween I was fifteen. The cops came," I sighed reminiscently, "and everything."

"Bitch went to her grave with fewer teeth than I have," my warm, friendly grandfather cackled.

"You engaged in a physical fight with a woman?"

"Slut should have kept her legs closed round a married man. 'Course," he added, looking at me, "your father always was a worthless bastard."

"As I recall, he got a fist in the face that night as well."

"And woulda got a boot in the ass! If the cops hadn't cuffed me by then."

"The arresting officer gave me a Charms Blo-Pop," I reminisced, "and took me over to stay with my mom. She got to read the police report." I stooped and kissed his wrinkled forehead. And handed him the Cub grocery bag, which was full of cans of Bud.

CHAPTER 12

"Who's here?" I asked, yawning as I strolled into the kitchen. Sinclair, once done laughing, had been in a rush to get back to the manse, for which I could not blame him. He'd snuck into the library to read the Book of the Dead, and I'd come to the kitchen to pretend I didn't know, and also for a smoothie.

"Here, what? *Here* here?" Marc was yawning, too, and scratching his ribs; he smelled like cotton balls, antiseptic, and was wearing last night's scrubs. His hair, shaved nearly bald when I met him, was now shoulder length, dark, and fell into his eyes a lot. It was a wonder how he examined anyone at the hospital. "I hate your creepy vampire superpowers."

"Liar."

"It's Nick," Jessica announced, shutting the fridge and turning around, a pomegranate (a pomegranate! She ate 'em like oranges, I swear to God) in her left hand.

"Oh."

I'd probably better leave. I had recently discovered that Detective Nick Berry, who was in love with my best friend, hated me. And not "hate" like "I hate boogers." Hated me like plague. Hated me like famine. The fact that I deserved it didn't make things any easier. "You guys have a date?"

"No," she said cryptically, which made me want to strangle her. When Jess didn't want to cough up, you could stick a gun in her ear, and she'd laugh at you. Must be from growing up rich. Sinclair was the same way. Stick a gun in *my* ear, and I'd talk until your pants fell down.

Then: "How's your grandpa?"

"Still worried that your blackness will infect me."

"That's the plan. First you, then all the other blondes, and then on to brunettes and redheads. Once we have the womenfolk, all the babies will come out black, too. We all voted on the plan at the last Black Conspirators meeting." Ignoring Marc's choking, she added, "Bet Sinclair had a good laugh."

"To put it mildly. He was all soft and nostalgic at first, talking about how it was nice to have live in-laws, but my grandpa wiped the smile off his face soon enough.

But never mind that. What's Nick doing here?"

"Meh," the Cryptic One replied.

"He's a carpenter by night? Not that we need one anymore; that gang you hired did a pretty good job." And they did. Except for the smell of sawned wood and fresh paint, you'd think nothing had happened.

"Yeah, thanks, Jessica. What do we owe you?" Now that I was married to a rich guy, I could say something like that and not have Jessica burst into derisive laughter. But as usual she just waved a hand: don't worry about it. I was so used to her money I hardly noticed it was there. Shit, *she* hardly knew it was there. But she was never obnoxious about it, seeing it as something permanent and unchangeable, like her skin color and taste in music.

"So," I continued, "not to go on and on about something —"

"You?" Marc asked.

"Never," Jessica declared.

I scowled at them both. "What *is* Nick doing here?"

"What do you care?" Marc asked, plucking an apple out of the basket on the counter and taking a wet bite. "He'd rather see you dead than in last year's Blahniks."

I shuddered and wiped masticated apple

off my cheek. "That was mean. Even for you."

"Obviously," Marc continued, shaking his hair out of his eyes (and into Jessica's pomegranate), "he and the richest woman in the state —"

"Richest *person*," Jessica corrected gently.

"— have a hot sloppy date. FYI, girlfriend, you're aware he's using you for your money, right?"

"His grandpa was one of the Deeres."

We gaped at her. This was a tidbit we hadn't heard before.

"Shut . . . *up!*" Marc nearly screamed.

"Nuh-uh." Jessica popped another pomegranate seed into her mouth and tried not to look smug. She sucked at it, as usual.

"As in the John Deere tractor company?" I advanced cautiously. (As in, anyone who wanted a tractor, trailer, thresher, or combine usually bought 'em from the John Deere Company.)

"Yup. He's got money falling out of his butt."

"Yum," Marc said absently.

I tried to speak for a couple of seconds and finally choked out, "Why didn't you tell us?"

"Why would I? What difference does it make if he's got a seven figure trust fund?"

"Well, it certainly makes him a more attractive man," Marc blurted before he could stop himself. "Also, money makes a guy's dick huge."

"Go fuck yourself," she said congenially enough.

"If only I could," he mourned. "It'd be the only way I'd get any, that's for sure."

The thing is, as exasperated as Marc and I were to be the last ones in on this incredibly juicy gossip (me more than him, probably, I mean, we *were* best friends), Jessica really meant what she said. She wouldn't know what difference it made, and wouldn't care.

It occurred to me that Sinclair had probably found this out ages ago and had also neglected to tell me. Must be a rich guy thing. Excuse me. Rich *person*. Not to mention, definitely the week for me to find out shit I should already have known.

"I'll get the door," I said gloomily, because I knew neither of them could hear Nick coming up the walk, and also because I decided the quickest way to find out why he was here was to let him in. As I started to leave the kitchen I nearly ran into my husband.

"I'm getting the door," I explained, trying to sidestep him.

He resisted, which made it like trying to sidestep a barn. "I'll accompany you."

I stared up at him. He must have died clean shaven. At least, I never saw him shaving, and there weren't any shaving — what was the word? accoutrements? — in his bathroom. God, he was gorgeous. Gorgeous and distant, like the sunrise he could never see. There were times I looked into that perfect, impassive face and wondered what he was thinking. Sometimes I was truly mystified: Out of all the vampires in all the world, why'd he want me?

We were still sidestepping each other in the hallway. "Why d'you want to come with me?"

"I'm unable to be outside of the goddess-like presence that is you?"

I heard Marc making vomiting noises as the kitchen door swung shut behind us. "No, seriously." Except with Sinclair, I never knew when he *was* serious.

"I miss you, and I want to be with you?"

"Come on."

"I am coming," he said, falling into step behind me.

"Yeah, this stopped being cute about five seconds ago."

"If only," my husband sighed.

"Sinclair, what the hell is up?"

"You have a meeting with Detective Berry, who has in the past threatened you with a firearm, and thus I will be in attendance as well. That is all."

"That is *all*?"

"Oh. Also, if he points a firearm anywhere near you, I shall pull off his arms and stuff them down his throat."

He said *that* just as I was swinging the front door open. "You will not! Jessica will be impossible to live with! (More impossible.)" Then: "Wait a damned minute! You knew about Nick coming to see me before I did, even if he tried to kill me?"

"Of course."

"You prick."

Nick, all annoying blond good looks and broad shoulders, smirked at us. For the first time, I noticed he dressed pretty damned well on a cop's salary. That was an Armani hanging off his swimmer's shoulders, if I wasn't mistaken.

"Did I come at a bad time?" he asked, grinning, and it took all I had not to slam the door in his stupid, rich, cop face.

CHAPTER 13

I should explain that before I died, Nick and I had been almost friends. When I'd been attacked by the Fiends outside Kahn's Mongolian Barbecue (the heavy garlic I'd used had saved my life; the Fiends had nibbled and fled instead of really going to town on my gizzard), he'd been the cop to take my report. We'd occasionally shared a candy bar and, if not friends, had at least been friendly.

Then I'd risen from the dead and, completely unaware of my undead sex appeal, left Nick panting after me. Sinclair had to mind-wipe him, including the part about me dying.

Trouble was, it wore off. Or my mind-wipe had been stronger than the king's. Either way, we found out a couple months ago that he knew what we were, knew what we did, knew what we had done to *him,* and pretty much hated us.

So out of guilt, I usually try to be super nice and accommodating whenever he came around.

Except, of course, right now.

"Nobody's having *any* meeting until you two *jerks* tell me when you set this up!"

Nick arched his brows at my husband. "You didn't tell her?"

"I was hoping," he said stiffly, "she would be out shoe shopping."

"Well, the joke's on you, *asshat!* Ha! I went shoe shopping last week! So there!" I jerked my pointing finger away from my husband and jabbed it at Nick, who flinched. "So talk! Are you here to kill me?" (Man, the number of times I had to ask this question in a month . . .)

"No, my captain said I couldn't, unless I could prove in court you were a vampire."

I nearly fell down in the foyer. "What?" I gasped, barely hanging on to the doorknob.

"Kidding. Come sit down before you stroke out." Nick pushed past us and, like robots, we followed him into one of the parlors.

Chapter 14

"So!" he said with faux brightness. "Set up a meeting with your wife, which you didn't share with your wife. I love open marriages, don't you?"

Since I'd been having some doubts in that area myself, all I could do was scowl at Sinclair while smiling at Nick, which gave me an instant migraine. "How can I help you, Nick? Did you want to see Jess? Oh, wait —" I should offer him a drink. But what *did* he drink? Was it Sprite, or Coke? Wait. *I* drank Coke. I —

"Detective Berry," Tina said demurely. She entered, eyes lowered, and offered him a tray on which were a tall glass full of Sprite, another glass full of ice, a silver ice picker-upper, a small bowl of sliced lemons and limes, and a big, thick, cloth napkin. Also, there was —

"My queen," she said in a soft voice, gaze on the carpet. I took the iced Coke (with a

77

wedge of lime, just the way I liked it), and Tina managed to somehow glide away while not looking at anyone, yet giving the impression of instant service, should anyone need a refill. This, I had since learned, was the height of vampiric etiquette. It's tough to do the vampire mojo and work your will on the poor human if you're not looking them in the eye.

I thirstily slurped my Coke, amazed all over again at Tina's unflagging efficiency. Super secretary, maid, waitress, Sinclair's right hand, and she'd been loyal to me from the moment the vampires threw me into Nostro's pit of despair. I couldn't help but admire her, but I never forgot the basic fact: her loyalty, always, was to Sinclair first. Her loyalty to me was because I was *his wife.*

The day I forgot that might be a short damn day.

"Good service around here," Nick said, slurping his Sprite and chewing enthusiastically on his lemon wedge.

"Oh, like you're not used to it at the Deere family compound," I snapped, chomping into my own lime slice. Yerrgh, sour! Even for a lime. I reached into my left pocket and pulled out a Cherry Blo-Pop. Unwrapped it, dipped it in the Coke, then contentedly sucked the Coke off the Pop.

"How disgusting," Sinclair commented.

"Which? That I'm slowly getting addicted to suckers, or that Nick comes from the Deeres?"

"Finally bothered to find out about someone besides yourself, huh?"

"Jam it up your ass!" I snarled, a not auspicious beginning to our meeting. And why were we meeting? He hated me, I was scared of him (but not for the reasons he thought), and Sinclair would just as soon he dropped dead (he took a dim view of cops shoving their service revolvers into his wife's face). "On the way out the door!"

"Hmm." Nick checked his watch. "Four minutes . . . a new record for us. Actually, Betsy, as I explained to the king of all suckheads over there, I need your help in tracking down a bad guy."

"You — me? Tracking down a — what?"

"English really is your second language, isn't it? And your suckhead is here because he's got this nutty idea that I'm going to try to shoot you in the face. Maybe twice!" he added cheerfully, slurping the last of his Sprite.

"Have a seat, Detective Berry." Sinclair looked up at me and patted his lap, and I ignored the tug between my legs because a meeting with a homicide detective while

79

curled up in the arms of the vampire king would not be the severe business mien I was hoping for. Bad enough I was wearing faded blue sweatpants and a sweatshirt that read EVERYTHING YOU'VE HEARD IS TRUE.

Instead, I plopped on the couch across from Nick (ignoring the plume of dust I accidentally raised), parallel to Sinclair.

"What's up, boys?" I asked, sniffing my Coke glass.

"Murder, of course." Crunch, slurp. He was really going to town on those lemons. "Check it."

He spun open several folders, and suddenly there were (gag) autopsy photos all over the Victorian-era mahogany coffee table. Thankfully, none were of children, but in all other ways they were different: race, sex, age, hairstyle.

"And how can the house of Sinclair help the Minneapolis Homicide Department?"

I opened my mouth (momentarily forgetting the lollipop; the thing almost fell on the floor), but decided I kind of liked that. House of Sinclair. Like House of Pancakes! Without so much syrup.

"Guess what all these guys (and gals) have in common?"

"They all need a set and shampoo," I said,

examining one photo and putting it down with a grimace. I wiped my fingers on my sweatpants, as if the picture had actually been dirty.

A year ago, I'd be sprinting from the room and vomiting. That was before Nostro, and Marjorie, and Alice, to name just a few. The guy who said "the more things change, the more things stay the same" had a major frigging head injury. Because I, Betsy, the vampire queen, am here to tell you that the more things change, the more things *change.*

"Close," Nick said, still looking abnormally cheery, "but no Kewpie doll for you, blondie."

Sinclair was also examining the photos. "They certainly weren't killed by vampires."

"True."

"Do we have to do the guessing thing?" I whined. "Just tell us."

"They all had records."

"Like, prison records?"

"Like, they were all thieves, rapists, killers."

No wonder he was so happy. Cops loved it when bad guys got killed.

"This is how you spend your evenings?" the Ant said behind my left shoulder, causing me to yelp and spill my ice all over Nick.

81

"Looking at disgusting pictures? This is worse than when you were modeling for the Target catalog."

"Go *away*. I'm working."

"Gaaahhh," Nick gah'd, frantically scraping ice out of his crotch. "What's gotten into you, blondie?"

"Private family business," Sinclair said smoothly.

"My dead stepmother is haunting me," I snapped. "Now get lost, Antonia!"

"Oh, that." Nick looked unimpressed. "You see dead people. Jess told me all about it."

"Well, that's super. Remind me to strangle her when I see her again."

"Touch her," Nick said pleasantly, "and I'll empty my nine into your nose."

"Children," Sinclair warned. "It seems the late Mrs. Taylor has a gift in death, as in life, of getting on my wife's nerves and distracting us from our point."

"Just like your wife!"

"Shut up," I insisted. "Tell us what you want, or get lost. Or both."

"Fine," the Ant huffed, and vanished.

Well! That was unexpected, and welcome.

"Guess what else all these guys have in common," Nick said, rattling my empty Coke glass. Tina appeared from nowhere, refilled it, and glided away. He absently handed the glass to me, and I didn't know whether to be flattered he'd noticed I needed a refill, or annoyed he was treating the brilliant Tina like she was a waitress. "Go on. Guess. You'll never guess."

"Since we'll never guess," Sinclair said, "why don't you just tell us?"

"Just *one* teensy guess?"

"Niiiiiick," I whined.

"Um. Ah. Hmm. They were all killed by a rogue cop or cops?" Sinclair inquired innocently.

We both stared at him.

"Goddammit," Nick cursed. He ignored, or didn't notice, Sinclair's flinch. "You gotta tell me how you knew that. I know for a fact there's no suckheads on the force."

"No, but there are sources available to the suckheads. As you well know, Detective Berry, nothing leaks more quickly or messily than a police station."

"So cops are tracking down bad guys and executing them?" I stared at the pictures. Gunshot wounds, all of them.

"The ones we can't put away legally, yeah. This guy." Dave tapped the photo of a pale, brown-eyed man who looked extremely pissed off, either because or in spite of the bullet wound over his left eye. "This guy

was a burglar, and worse. He'd rape who-
ever was asleep in the house — we think he
was getting the security codes from someone
inside the security company, but he, uh,
died before we could prove anything."

"Charming," Sinclair said coldly.

"Anyway, after the rape, he'd take everything out he could carry. We know he did it
seven or eight times, but couldn't ever prove
it. No ID. No prints. No semen. Nothing.
Then — bam. He shows up deader than
hell."

"And your problem with this is . . . ?"
Sinclair's dark brows arched.

"Because the cops are good guys," I said
before Nick could reply. "I mean, it sucks if
they can't catch a rapist, jeez, you won't
hear me argue that, but we have *laws*. We
have *rules*. The good guys can't all of a sudden throw the Constitution out the window
and strap down and shoot people."

I looked at Sinclair and Nick, who had
identically blank looks on their faces. "Well.
They *can't*."

"As it is, I agree with the psycho vampire
queen. Which brings me here."

"Why does the house of Sinclair have to
clean up your mess?" my husband asked
quietly.

"It's like your wife said. We make various

84

promises and pledges when we get our badges — I won't bore a sociopath like you with them — but what it boils down to is, we follow the law. And boys and girls, Sherri's boy Nicky loves the law."

"Don't you have a special team or task force or whatever working on this?"

"Yeah. I'm it."

"You? Just one guy? I mean, I know you're good at your job, Nick, but —"

"Well, let's say I have some influence with the captain." Nick mimed driving a tractor.

"No doubt. And, could it be, the police do not necessarily wish for these people to be caught?"

"It could be," he admitted. "But they're gonna get caught. 'Cause I've got a secret weapon." He pointed at me.

"What makes you think — oh, shit, never mind, you know I'll do it."

"That's true." Nick smirked. "I did know it."

CHAPTER 15

"You should let him solve his own problem," Sinclair said in a low voice, as Nick let himself out. "He's playing on your misplaced guilt."

"Misplaced? We *raped* his *brain.* And lied about it. To his face. For over a year."

He shrugged. He'd been a vampire too long; his conscience went right out the window sometimes.

"Have you ever considered —"

"Yes."

"Don't be a wiseass. Have you ever thought that the guy hates us and knows how to kill us, but hasn't?"

"I credit Jessica with that more than Detective Berry's good sense."

"Point," I conceded. "And yeah, it's a little obnoxious that he came over all expecting me to say yes right away —"

"Also, you're flattered."

"I am not! Okay, a little. Listen, this is our

chance to win him back!"

"And why," he sighed, rubbing my shoulders, while I tried not to purr and lean into him, "would we want to do that?"

"Listen. Oooh, don't stop. The whole reason you pushed Jess to go out with him was because you wanted a source in the police department." I paused. "Another source, I mean. That reminds me. You've been keeping secrets. More than usual, I mean."

"Oh?" he said silkily, tightening his grip. My collarbones groaned under the pressure. Or maybe that was me groaning. "Because there are one or two things I would like to discuss with you as well, if you're opening that door."

"Ahhhh . . . well, that's, um —" Fortunately, I was saved by the sound of splintering wood, and then Nick skidded down the foyer, his face a mask of blood.

"Face us, false queen!"

"Oboy," I said, nearly tripping as Sinclair grabbed me and thrust me behind his back. "That doesn't sound good."

CHAPTER 16

They streamed in, stepping smoothly over Nick's unconscious body. They moved like cats and had the hungry, feral look of same. At least, as far as I could tell from peeking over Sinclair's shoulder; I kept trying to elbow him out of the way, and he kept jamming me behind him.

"Uh, hi. You'd be, um, Garrett's friends, right?"

Happy, Skippy, Trippy, Sandy, Benny, Clara, and Jane glared at me as one. Somewhere, they'd clothed themselves — probably at the farm, I was seeing an awful lot of flannel — but still had the rank smell of the unwashed. They were all too thin, even bony. Their hair was varying colors and degrees of snarled.

"Well," I plunged, "I'm sorry I wasn't here when you stopped by the other night —"

They weren't moving. Perhaps I was dazzling them with my ineptitude. It had happened before.

"But at least this gives me a chance to, um, explain and even, um, apologize —"

"Do *not* apologize to them," Sinclair snarled. "One such as you should not even speak to them."

"Shush! He's cranky," I explained, "no blood tonight, you know how it is."

"We know exactly how it is," Clara said.

"Oh. Right." Awkward. What was interesting wasn't their reaction so much as Sinclair's. He wasn't angry so much as — as — *offended,* that was the word. Their presence offended him. I guess the Fiends were the vampire untouchables.

"Anyway, the thing is, it has been a *crazy* couple of years. For me, I mean. First there was the whole 'you are the queen' thing, which I was so *not* prepared for. And, I might point out, a lot of people were telling me to kill all you guys when Nostro — when you ate Nostro — but I didn't. In fact, I *saved* you."

"For imprisonment and slow starvation."

"I'm *getting* to that." I lowered my voice. "Okay, so then there was a serial killer — more than one, come to think of it — and then my half sister turned up, who was the daughter of the devil. The devil! I mean, please!"

"Yes, please," one of them said. "Let us end this."

"But I'm not finished! And then — before then, actually — all these ghosts started showing up looking for favors, like in that movie? Never mind, you didn't see that movie."

One of them was rubbing her temples. I sped up the This Is My Life portion of our program. "Then my friend got sick, lethally sick, and I had this wedding to plan, and all these werewolves showed up, and my dad and step mom died because I wanted a baby, and I had to kill a librarian, and it was just — just a crazy, crazy time. I mean, totally nuts."

"So. Essentially," Sandy — or was it Benny? — said, "you forgot about us."

"Well."

"Do not," Sinclair said through gritted teeth.

"Kinda," I admitted. "But I had all these really good reasons! I — yeek!" Sinclair had shoved me into the curtains as seven enraged vampires launched themselves at me.

CHAPTER 17

It's hard to even describe the fight. With enhanced strength, speed, and reflexes, everything happened so fast, and then it was all over but the bandaging.

The first one that got near Sinclair dropped, and so did the next one. One got past him and got a good grip on my hair (must have been a female killed in the 1920s . . . that was the hair-pulling era, right?), but I brought my head forward in a blur of coolness and broke her nose with a satisfying crunch. The blow made me stagger, and I wiped her blood off my forehead . . . sluggish, nasty dark stuff.

And the screaming! All the screaming! Wait. Only one person was screaming. *Marc* was screaming.

I shoved Hair Puller at the fireplace, peripherally noticing the ceramic tiles rain down on her stupid face as she hit the floor. Then I ran toward the shrieking Marc, who was on his back fighting off flashing fangs and teeth (Clara? Benny? It was going so quickly I couldn't tell).

Before I could get to them, Tina leaned over them, grabbed Clara/Benny *by the hair* and yanked him (ah, a guy, I saw it now) off Marc. She had something long and shiny in her other hand, and I recognized it, as she swung the Wusthof butcher knife (Jessica's pride and joy, she had a whole collection in the butler's pantry, and they were wicked sharp), hard enough to decapitate Benny. His headless body fell with a thump, and Marc scrambled back on his hands, so the thing wouldn't fall on him.

Tina had dropped the head and was turning to see who else she could decapitate, when a wooden spoon burst through her chest.

"This?" the Ant demanded. "This is how you spend your time? Squabbling with people who don't bathe?"

"Not . . . *now!*" I ran to Tina, nearly tripping over the body of a Fiend Sinclair had killed, and yanked the serving spoon out of her heart. Then I grabbed her head and screamed into her eyes, which had begun to gloss over. "Don't you *dare* die on me, you efficient bitch, don't you *dare!*"

"I — I'm fine. I'm all right, my queen."

We both looked down. The wooden serving spoon, about nine inches long, was now ash. I had turned it to ash. And Tina was all right.

No, I didn't know how.

And then the door was slamming, the other Fiends were gone, and the fight was over.

CHAPTER 18

We'd killed two of them: Sinclair had killed Trippy; Tina had killed Benny. Marc was wounded, bleeding like the proverbial stuck pig, but it looked mostly superficial. Jessica, who had been keeping a terrified Garrett from fleeing down the tunnel, drove Marc to the ER. Marc's last delirious comment was, "Will I become a vampire now? Cool!"

By then, the rest of the Fiends had fled, and Nick had regained consciousness. "Yeah, that'll show 'em," he said groggily, as he caromed from one wall to another, trying to stagger out the door. It looked like he had a broken nose, but I hoped that was the worst of it. We offered to call an ambulance, but he tagged along with Jessica, who I knew would tell him the whole story.

Sinclair carried Tina upstairs to the hot tub room, dunked her in (over her protests; we were pretty sure I'd cured the wound), and, after ten minutes, let her out.

About the water thing: for some reason, when vampires are grievously hurt, water speeds up the healing process. I had no idea why. Maybe because our undead bodies didn't have much moisture? I didn't know. So much of being a vampire was like magic to me. And not the cool kind, either.

Tina shook the wet hair out of her eyes and grinned at me. "Two down. Five to go."

"You were nuts, launching yourself at that guy."

"You and the king had your hands full," she said dryly. I handed her a robe, and she snuggled into it. Not a mark on her, thank God.

"But you were stabbed with wood," Sinclair said, looking ashen. "I saw it."

Tina looked at me, and I winked. So she shrugged and said to the king, "It must have missed my heart."

Oooooh, she's actually lying to the king of the vamps! Somebody write down the date and time. And I had to admit, it was nice to be the one keeping secrets for a change.

"But I *saw* —"

"Come on," I sighed. "Let's make smoothies. Or something."

CHAPTER 19

We visited Marc later that night. Sure, two o'clock in the morning isn't considered optimum visiting hours, but this wasn't the first late-night trip to this hospital for me. Or even the tenth. I knew who to sidestep, who to put the vampire mojo on, and who didn't give a tin shit if Bin Laden was on the floor, as long as he or she could snag an extra hour of sleep in the on-call room.

"Disgusting," Marc informed me cheerily from his bed, as he played with the tilt settings and television remote control at once. "This hospital's about as secure as the men's rooms in the Target Center. But thanks for coming to see me so fast."

"After my second smoothie, you were all I could think about."

"Tell the truth," he said soberly. "My hair looks awful, doesn't it?"

"Well . . ." If he considered most of the hair on the right, which was clotted with blood and hopelessly snarled to be awful, then . . . "At least you've got your health. Oh, wait."

"Aren't you funny." He stretched out his bandaged arms and looked at them. After being stitched up (fifteen stitches in his left arm, twenty-six in his right, thirty-one in his right leg, eighteen in the muscle just below his right nipple, seven stitches to the left of his belly button), he'd been admitted for overnight observation. "It looked worse than it was, in case you were wondering."

"Actually, I was wondering if you could pull the blanket up a little more."

"Oh." Marc was still staring down at himself, but had yet to notice he was naked.

"I'll, uh, just do that." I bustled around the bed, trying to make myself useful.

He looked pleased. "Now I'm tucked in!"

For the first time I realized his green-eyed gaze was a little cloudy. I peered closer. So did he. Our faces were about an inch apart but, again, Marc didn't seem to think this was at all unusual.

"Jeez," I said, so close my breath (if I had any) would have fogged his glasses (if he wore them). "How much medication are you on?"

"Well, let's see. I had some Valium at the house, and some more on the way to the hospital. (I offered some to Nick, but he said no thanks.) Then in the ER, the intern said —"

"You know what? It doesn't matter. As long as you're okay is all."

"Oh, sure! I'm great! You know, for someone who was trying to kill me, he mostly just knocked me down and got me dirty. I mean, did you *see* those guys? Covered with mud!"

"Yeah, that's annoying." I fought not to roll my eyes or sneak a peek at the clock on the wall.

"I think he wanted to kill you and was mostly trying to get me out of his way. I'll be sore and itchy for ages, and I'll have spec*tacular* bruising, and maybe a couple of really butch scars, but that's the extent of it. I feel pretty lucky."

"I'm — I'm glad, Marc." He *had* been lucky, but I was mostly too tormented by guilt. And hunger pangs. I was so thirsty, and the smells generated by the hospital were making me drool. As the queen, I didn't have to feed every night like all the other vampires, and sometimes I made the mistake of pushing it. It had been at least four days. "Also, don't come back."

He absently cracked his knuckles; they sounded like Rice Crispies. "Yep, after tonight it'll be smooth — what?"

"You can't come back until we take care of this Fiend situation."

"Take care of the situation? You're talking like it's a termite infestation!"

"If only," I muttered. "Look, I feel crummy that you got hurt, but you *were* lucky, and I'm not enough of a twit to put you right back in danger."

He blinked at me slowly, like an owl, and I could tell he was trying to muster an argument. After a long silence he said, "But we have the Super Secret Vampire Tunnels to escape to."

"Yeah, except every one of the Fiends is faster than you and Jess, and what if they cut you off next time? What if Sinclair and I, God forbid, aren't even home next time?"

"But we can —"

"Marc, I'm sorry, I guess I didn't realize . . . you think this is a debate. It's not. You *could* run to the tunnels, Sinclair and I *might* be able to protect you, the Fiends might come back *but* not try to hurt you . . . whatever, man. Too many maybes for me — you're out."

"But Betsy . . ." His eyes filled, and he shook his head savagely, making the tears fly. Then he was glaring at me with wet cheeks. "That's my *home,* same as it is yours. Where can I go?"

"Yeah, about that." Marc wasn't seeing anyone right now (he'd had a fling a month or so ago, but otherwise was something of a dateless wonder), and no family — at least, none he would ever live with ever again. "Where do you want to go? You pick the place, and Sinclair will pay for it. Sinclair and I," I corrected, since technically it was now my fortune, too.

"I don't want to pick anything," Marc began, still pissed, but then I could see the possible advantages of the situation begin to trickle past the fog of drugs. "Uh. Anywhere I want?"

"Anywhere. Until we fix this. The day the Fiends pack it up and go home" — Yeah, sure, that's how this would end — "is the day you move back in."

An expression of vague alarm crossed his features. "But what if the Fiends stay out of sight for, I dunno, two years? Before they make their move? Are you going to keep me out of my home for *years?*"

"It won't come to that." And try as I might, I just couldn't picture it. Not to be all egotistical or anything, but I couldn't imagine the Fiends could do much of anything until they'd settled with me. Laying back in the buckwheat for a couple of years was definitely not their style. "It absolutely won't. But right now it's too dangerous for you. Of course it's your home, and the day the Fiends are taken care of is the day you come back. But until then . . ."

I tucked another blanket around Marc and left him sleepily murmuring, "The Radisson? No. The Millennium? No. Sofitel? I know! The Grand! Will they do turndown service for me . . . ?"

CHAPTER 20

As Marc's door was wheezing shut behind me, I heard Jessica trotting toward me. I was able to pick up the sound of her footsteps over everyone else's in the hall (granted, at this hour, there weren't many, but still — my very own stupid pet trick!) and turned in time for her to wave to get my attention.

It seemed to take a very long time for her to get to me. Sinclair and I had talked about this phenomenon once or twice, after making love. It was starting to seem more and more natural, taking advantage of my vampiric senses and all. In the beginning, they either overwhelmed me (especially when I was hungry) or I had to sit still and make a conscious effort to hear, to smell, to whatever outside the range of normal human activity. Now I could probably pick Sinclair or Jess or Mom out of a Metrodome crowd.

Now her mouth was moving, verrrry

sloooooowly. I squinted at her and then yelped when she pinched me.

"Sorry, but you had a very goofy look on your face. How is he? Is he sleeping?"

"He's a little out of it."

"Oh." She stared at the closed door as if she had suddenly developed X-ray vision and could, y'know, actually see what was happening on the other side. "Do you think I should go in? It's so late. Think he'd be mad if I didn't come in tonight? I don't think he'd be mad. And I'll see him tomorrow. I'll bring him some Bruegger's for breakfast. Let's walk. Can we walk? Come on."

I didn't say a word, just fell into step beside her. It wasn't hard to figure out why she was nervous — she had, after all, spent many days in this very hospital as a terminal patient. That'd take the shine off your night, even if the other events hadn't.

I cut through her nervous chatter as we headed to the hospital parking ramp. "Actually, you could help me out *and* radically reduce your trips to the hospital."

"Sing it."

"Well, we're putting Marc up somewhere nice, sort of as a treat, you know? I mean, he's been through a *lot*. He was finally starting to date again but he had that bad breakup last month . . . and he's been picking up so many extra shifts . . . and he really got torn up tonight."

"Yeah," Jessica said slowly, "I guess you could say he's had a crummy few weeks."

"Right!" She was falling for it! The puny human had no hope whatsoever of overcoming the mightiness that was me, Betsy, vampire queen and recovering Miss Congeniality. "So maybe you could go with him, wherever he picks, and sort of settle him in, you know? Make sure he's got everything he needs, and —"

Jessica had stopped walking, which was awkward, as I didn't immediately notice, and I have long legs and walk fast, so I had to walk all the way back across the skyway if I wanted to keep participating in the conversation. Which, judging by her thunderous expression, I did not.

"Betsy. Oh my God. How —"

— did I know that was just what Marc needed? How could we best help him get settled? How did I manage to say the right thing time and time again?

Naw. I knew the tone and I knew it wasn't going to be good.

"— fucking dumb do you think I am?"

"You mean, on a sliding scale, or —"

"You've gotten rid of one human, and now

you're trying to ditch the other."

"Oh, say, hey now! I think 'ditch' is a little — ow."

She had jammed her index finger into the middle of my chest and now poked to emphasize her words. With each poke a cloud-colored fingernail jabbed me. It was like being pricked over and over again with the world's dullest needle. We'd had so many fights like this, I practically had scars there. "I'm. Not. Going. Anywhere. Besides, it's my house! You can't kick me out of —"

"Also, Sinclair wants to buy it from you. I mean, we want to buy it. The house. We totally do. Together. It's not just him alone. *We* want to." Because that's what married couples did, right? Bought real estate together and drank each other's dark, dead blood?

"Oh, I'll just *bet* you do." She pulled her small, sleek head back, like a snake getting ready to bite. It was silly, kind of: I was a foot taller, I was thirty pounds heavier, I had legions of the Undead at my command (sorta) and vampiric strength, and I was scared to death of her. I tried not to cower as she ranted, "Well, you can't have it! For one thing, it's not for sale, and for another, it's my house!"

"Jessica, we almost lost you this summer,

and —"

"Betsy, even if you couldn't cure cancer, I wouldn't be afraid of the Fiends. But hey! Since you can? I can't say I'm worried about something as silly as a few bites."

We started walking again, only she was stomping toward the elevator, and I was doing the Igor Shuffle ("Yes, master, right away, master, I am not an animal, master.") right behind her. "A few bites? That's like calling the cost of the War on Terror a few dollars. And I know you're not afraid, it's not about you being afraid, it's about taking the sensible precaution of being elsewhere when the bad guys come back, doy!"

She snorted and jabbed the elevator button. "Listen to you. 'Sensible precautions.' "

"And don't forget the 'doy.' Jess, how many scary movies have we seen where the heroine does something really dumb like hang around in a hallway when she knows the bad guys are, like, a room away?"

" 'Bout a zillion," she acknowledged.

"We got off *real* lucky this time — Marc with a few scratches, and you not even hurt — and I think it's completely nuts to push it. So how about you don't be an asshole about it and just stay with Marc until we kill all the bad guys?"

"Oh, someone's being an asshole," she

agreed, practically leaping into the elevator in her agitation, "but it's not this girl."

I leaned against the wall and closed my eyes. Mostly against the awful fluorescents in the elevators; there were about eight too many. "I knew you were gonna be like this."

"But you had to open your yap anyway."

I squinted at her. "Don't come crying to me when a Fiend tears your head off."

She smiled a little, and I knew that was partly because she thought she had won the argument. She hadn't, but she was forcing me to do something I really, really, really didn't want to do.

I was gonna tell on her.

CHAPTER 21

I nearly walked through the Ant on my way from the bathroom to the bed, and neither of us were very happy about the near miss.

"Must you ignore everyone's personal boundaries?"

"Yeeeeeggghh! Stop *doing* that, you disgusting horrible dead wretch!"

Sinclair, all the way across the room, looked guilty and bent down to untie his other Kenneth Cole, as opposed to just yanking it off and tossing it in the general direction of the closet.

"You might think about what would happen to me if you got your silly self killed."

"Yeah, I should have realized what a terrible thing that would be, Ant. *For you.*" I ran the six steps from the bathroom, jumping into the middle of the bed, so nothing hiding under it could grab my feet. "And I wasn't talking to you," I added to my husband, "but it's nice to see you treating your shoes with more respect."

The Ant was looking in our direction with rabid suspicion. Which, since she'd been heavily Botox'd before her death, came across as slightly raised eyebrows and rapidly blinking eyes. "What are you two doing? You're not going to bed *now?*"

"We've been up all night, you pineapple-colored idiot." Pineapple referring to her hair, which was stiff and yellow. "Dawn's about an hour away."

"Well, in that time you could be —"

"Having nasty sex with my husband. Nasty," I added, ignoring Sinclair as he picked up a pillow, calmly pressed it over his face, and barked laughter into it. "With, um, probes and things. We like to role-play. I'm the alien, and he's the helpless probed human. Now get lost, because it's going to get messy in here."

Ah! It worked. She'd popped out while I was horrifying her with lurid descriptions of my imaginary sex life. I wish she'd just tell me what she wanted and go back to Hell already.

"Thank" — I searched for a word that wouldn't make Sinclair cringe — "goodness she's gone."

"Help, help, I'm being probed!" The pillow sailed at my head, and I knocked it away, trying not to grin. Beside me, Sinclair tried his best to look horrified. "If only I didn't feel a sick, wrong sexual attraction to these alien invaders. If only I had listened to my mother's warnings about loose alien women!"

"Pal, you are so not getting any tonight."

"If only," he continued dolefully, "they didn't keep telling me to turn my head and cough."

That was it; I lost it. I shrieked and laughed and kicked at the covers until the bed looked like what I told the Ant we'd be up to.

"That was slightly . . . hysterical."

"Hey, it's been a long night."

"Indeed it has, my darling alien intruder." Sinclair yanked the remaining sheets and blankets off the bed and threw them to the floor with a theatrical flourish. Then he pounced on me while sheets billowed all over the place.

He kissed me for a wonderfully long time, then pulled back and cocked an eyebrow. "Want to see my probe?"

CHAPTER 22

The next evening started off nice and quiet. Marc wasn't around, of course, Garrett was probably still cowering in the basement, and I didn't look too hard for Jessica.

Almost as soon as I'd gotten up, Tina and Sinclair had left for the library. This made sense, as the former librarian, Marjorie, had kept extensive files on every vampire she knew of, heard of, or could track down.

Information, as far as the late, unmourned Marjorie believed, had been power.

They had politely asked if I wanted to come, pretending I'd actually be of use to a couple of near geniuses trapped in a warehouse disguised as a library. They probably thought hours of research on computers and — and whatever you did research on would be a good time, poor morons. Of course I'd said no.

But even if I'd lost all my cool points and was a hopeless, helpless virgin weirdo geek who *wanted* to spend half the night in a vampire library, I couldn't.

I, after all, had serious work to do for the Minneapolis Police Department. Make that Homicide Department. Yeah, that's right, we vampire queens are in constant demand all over the place for —

"Are you actually going to get in my car?" Nick Berry demanded, shaking his keys at me. "Or just keep staring off into space like that? Because it is fuckin' creepy, Betsy, you look like the Exlax is about to kick in."

"Huh? Oh. That was mean. And I'm *coming,* don't *nag.*"

"I'm a grown man," he forced out through gritted teeth, "and we don't nag."

"You were! You *were* nagging!"

"Betsy, I swear to God, if you don't shut your fucking yap and get in the car, I'm going to pull out my gun and blow your —"

"Ha! You said 'blow.' "

The gun had cleared the holster. Hmm, Nick was a short-tempered fellow these days. "I'm gonna count to ten. One. Seven. Nine. T—"

"Hold it right there!"

We both jumped like we'd been caught doing something nasty, and looked. Jessica the Terrible was stomping down the porch and across the driveway toward us.

Quick as thought, Mr. Gun was back in his house, Mr. Holster.

"Hi, babe, I thought you were sleeping."

"Oh, Jess. I didn't know you were up."

"Well?" She stopped, slightly out of breath. She must have sprinted when she figured out Nick was here. "Which is it? I'm in bed asleep because I have a human boyfriend, or I'm wide awake because my best friend is a vampire?"

"Uh —"

"You're so great," Nick said warmly. "It's both."

Man, I could never pull that off.

"You sneaky lying sack of shit."

Apparently Nick couldn't, either.

"You're sneaking off with him to — well, I don't know what, but I don't like it. And you!" She rounded on Nick, jabbing with the dreaded index finger (which was now painted eggplant). "I know damn well you don't like being alone with Betsy anymore. So what are you up to?"

He didn't tell her?

"You didn't tell her?" I tried to hide my delight at Nick's look of consternation . . . and the fact that it bummed me out, hearing Nick was scared to be alone with me. At least I wasn't the only one who was scared to death of Pissed Off Jessica — hell, he was *armed,* and he looked ready to sidle around the corner and hide. "That's awful. Why wouldn't you tell her?"

"Because she'll jump to the conclusion that I'm trying to get you killed," he snapped.

"Yeah, she's funny that way."

"What? Get killed? Why might you get killed? Betsy, you can't go off doing something dangerous with Nick, when those disgusting Fiends could be back any minute and try to finish what —" Then she shut her mouth with a snap.

Nick and I looked at each other, then at Jessica. I felt sorry for her. She really did try to keep Nick out of the vampire stuff, telling him only what she absolutely thought he needed to know.

And of course, she didn't get into the gory details of Nick's terror and hatred of me, just made the occasional reference to it. She was a good dancer. And it was too bad she had to dance at all. I mean, more than the normal amount any best friend does when balancing a lifelong friendship with a new love affair.

"Why don't we get in the car," I suggested, "and Jess goes back in the house, and the three of us pretend the last forty-five seconds never happened."

"Deal."

"Deal."

Nick started up his SedanMobile as I waved to Jess, who was back on the porch and anxiously waving back.

"Betsy! Let's go!"

"Your car," I told him, gingerly climbing into the front seat, "smells like ass."

CHAPTER 23

"Man, that was bad. We coulda handled that one better. A lot better."

"What are you talking about, 'we'? I'm not the one who completely screwed that one up. Hey, Jess gets full disclosure from me, pal."

"Oh fucking bullshit," he snapped, almost running down a squirrel. He turned onto Grand Avenue, where he'd have better luck with hapless pedestrians. "You told me yourself after that — after that business around your wedding that you kept her out of the vampire stuff."

"After I cured her terminal illness, you mean? Is that what you're referring to?" My voice was so sugary it would have given a diabetic an instant attack. I normally wouldn't bring it up, especially since I had no idea how I'd done it, but hey, Nick was bigger than me, and smarter. And armed. And he hated me. "Sure, Sinclair and I keep her out of it — keep her out in the sense of actually, physically keeping her out of it. But I still *tell* her everything."

"Nnmph," he grunted. Then, "Put on your seat belt."

"Please. Would you really give a gold-plated crap if I was launched screaming through your windshield?"

"State law."

Oh. Right. I, the Minnesota law-abiding vampire queen, obediently buckled up.

"She's got enough to worry about," he finally (lamely) said.

"You big liar! You're using me to ramp your solve rate, and I might get hideously mangled or killed. *That's* what you don't want her to 'worry' about."

"Ramp my solve rate?" He slid over two streets and merged onto I-94. "Betsy, stop watching *NYPD Blue* reruns."

"I don't! On purpose."

He groaned. "Please don't explain that."

"But Marc has a big crush on Sipowicz, and he's always hoping to see the man's butt again, and I can't help it if every time I go into the TV room or his room or one of the parlors, he's playing the DVDs."

"Well, if you're so damn sure I'm up to no good, how come you're here?"

"You know why."

"Enlighten me."

"Stop it."

"C'mon, I'm serious."

I stared at him. He stared back with his blank cop's face. Truth? Lie? Somewhere in between? I bet he could take a polygraph and never, what was the cop phrase? Never bounce a needle.

"I'm here to prove to you that I'm no danger to you, that we could be friends if you didn't shrivel with horror at the thought, that vampires can be good guys, too." I said it all in a rush, and it came out sounding like my drunken Marilyn Monroe impersonation.

"Yeah, you're going to have to slow that one down and run it by me again.

"I'm. Here. To. Prove. That. I'm. No. Danger. And. We. Can. Be. Friends. If. You. Didn't. Shrivel."

"That's okay, I think I can piece together the rest. Trouble is, blondie, why should I ever believe anything you tell me, ever again?"

"Oh, jeez!" I threw my hands up in the air. "How long are you going to hold that one thing against us? I've told you and told you, I was a new vampire and didn't know the rules!"

"Yeah, so you fucking mind-raped me."

I noticed that, like me, he tended to swear more when he was nervous or mad.

"Anything sounds bad when you say it like that," I conceded sulkily, staring out the passenger window.

He made a sound that might have been a snort, or a muffled laugh. When I looked, he had his cop face back on.

"So where are we going?"

"What a tactful, yet subtle way to change the subject."

"Fine. Don't tell me. Keep being the biggest, most gigantickest asshole —"

"Gigantickest?" he said, delighted. "Are you using word-a-day toilet paper again? Okay, okay, don't pout. And don't enlighten me about vampire toilet habits, I don't think I could stand it. I've managed to run down a couple of leads and thought I'd bring my favorite dead enforcer with me to see what's what."

"I thought you said your vigilante killer was a cop? Or cops, plural?"

"I did."

"So how can we check on them without, I dunno, scaring them? Tipping them off?"

"Very carefully. I've been running down when the murders took place — best as the M.E. can tell us, anyway — with the duty logs of the ones I think might be capable of something like this."

"Oh." That was really smart. And just laced with common sense. Exactly why I never would have thought of it. God, I'd be the *worst* police officer. I knew that about myself, had always known it, which was why it was kind of a thrill to be in a police car (the front seat, anyway), helping solve murders. Well. Coming along for the ride while someone else solved murders. "Huh. Okay."

"Do you know much about guns, Betsy?" He indicated his service piece. "If you're ever in a situation where you need to shoot a guy to save my ass, could you do it?"

"Wait. Do you hate me now because I'm a ruthless vampire who has killed before, or do you hate me because I'm a careless dimwit who can't be trusted with this power?"

"You mean, right now? Right this minute, why do I hate you?" he asked in a voice that was almost — so close! — teasing. "Do I have to choose? God, so many choices . . ."

"I don't have a lot of use for handguns," I said after a glance at the pistol at his waist. "Mostly I know about shotguns from goose hunting with my mom, and rifles for target practice."

"The professor hunts?"

"The professor can shoot the eye out of a squirrel at two hundred yards. I'll tell you who knows a ton about guns — Tina. She's an expert. You should get with her sometime."

"No thanks," he said curtly, and just like that, our fragile whatever it was came to an end.

CHAPTER 24

Nick dropped me off at about two-thirty in the morning, not remotely discouraged, although it looked to me like his leads hadn't panned out. At least he was being (relatively) friendly again, so I didn't say anything to wreck it. I just waved good-bye and trudged into the mansion.

Where a grim Sinclair and a fretful Jessica were waiting for me.

"Whaaaat?" I whined, moodily pulling off my Herrera boots. "What'd I do? I didn't do it. I'm pretty sure it was Marc. No, wait. Cathie!" Cathie, the ghost-gone-walkabout, who I could actually use to help me with the aunt. She was usually convenient for blame. Of course, if she'd been there, I never would have gotten away with it.

She'd been killed by a serial killer (who was later killed by my sister, Laura, who had a spectacular temper tantrum in the killer's basement) and, even after his death, had hung around being my ghostly secretary of sorts. If ghosts showed up needing help, Cathie would try to help them herself . . . and only if she couldn't would she then let the ghost bother me. Plus, she was super funny and nice. I missed having her around. Even more so now that the Ant was pestering me.

"Sinclair told me," Jessica said without preamble.

"About what?" I asked, totally at a loss. Man, I'd have to drink some blood soon. I was getting dumber by the hour.

"About Nick's little murder project," she said grimly, and I winced.

"That wasn't nice," I said to Sinclair, the reproach quite clear in my tone.

" 'Nice' is the least of my concerns, or interests. He is trying to get you killed, or at least cares not if you're hurt. If I could tell his superior without jeopardizing our secret, I would."

"You'd tattle to his boss! Oooh, that's *really* mean." I walked into the parlor and carefully flopped down onto a fainting couch, which someone had probably lugged over on the *Mayflower.*

"I'll deal with him later," she swore, and I almost felt sorry for the guy. "I just wanted to make sure you got back all right."

"Sure I did. Heck, it didn't even pan out. It was an evening of driving around, basically. Feel bad for *him,* he was the one trapped in a car with me." In fact, a couple of times he had rolled his window down and hung out his head like a dog, screaming into the wind. Heh.

"And I," Sinclair said, "wished to attempt to convince you, once again, to leave police matters to the police. We have other things to attend to."

"Oh, like I would have been any help to you and Tina tonight."

Sinclair lifted his left shoulder up about half a centimeter, which, for him, was the same as a shrug of agreement.

"Like I said, it was one big safe boring evening. No problems. And," I added, looking around the small, peach-colored parlor, "I assume the Fiends haven't been back?"

"No, thank God."

"Did you and Tina learn anything?"

"Oh, this and that," Sinclair said vaguely, which either meant (a) he had gobs of tidbits he didn't want to spill in front of Jessica, (b) he had nothing, or (c) he had plenty, but didn't want to worry me.

"So. Let's go to bed?"

"Do that," Jessica muttered, turning around like a soldier doing an about-face and marching out of the parlor. "I've got to call Nick."

"Very, very mean," I told my husband, as I followed him up the stairs. "Ratting Nick out like third graders squealing about who stole the chocolate milk. Nice!"

Sinclair shrugged again. I pulled our bedroom door shut and jumped on his back.

"Ah?" he managed, looking around for his suit hanger.

"I'm *starving*," I purred into his left ear.

The hanger, which he had just picked up, went sailing over our right shoulders. Then he reached back, got my coat in a fist, and yanked me off of him, *over* him, and flopped me onto the bed.

"Then let's eat," he said, and fell upon me like a scary fairy-tale monster, only a whole lot sexier and, let's face it, better dressed.

CHAPTER 25

The sun fell down the next night, but I'd been awake for about an hour by the time it was full dark. Still wasn't taking my increasing resilience to sunlight for granted, and still not trying to rub it in to Tina and Sinclair who were, after all, much older than I was.

I knew it was a real treat to be able to go for a walk outside in the late afternoon. I'd paid for it, though, thanks to the Faustian bargain that was the Book of the Dead. (Sinclair lost a bet once when he didn't think I knew what *Faustian* meant; but there's more than one way for a girl to Google a cat.)

I got dressed, then remembered what I'd forgotten last night. Amazing what good sex and half a pint of vampire king blood could do to jog your memory.

I flopped onto the bed, picked up the bedside phone, and dialed Nick.

"Homicide, Detective Berry."

"This is the woman," I purred in my throatiest voice, "who is going to make all of your dreams come true."

"Aunt Marian?"

"Gross!" I nearly dropped the phone. "Nick, that's disgusting!"

"So is your sexy voice. You sound like Patrick Warburton with a head cold. What's on your microscopic mind?"

"I forgot to tell you something last night."

"Of course you did. You're a dimwit."

"It's something that will make you extremely happy," I wheedled.

"You're moving, and you can't remember your forwarding address."

"You wish."

"The mailman left a hand grenade in your slot?"

"Do you want me to tell you, or do I have to listen to more dumb comments?"

"They are not dumb. So. What is it?"

"Nothing much. A cadre of old vampires is ticked at me, has already tried to kill me once, and won't stop until I'm dead or they are, and there's, like, twenty of them and only one of me. Also, we're out of milk."

"Really?" Nick sounded like he'd won the lottery. "You wouldn't tease me, would you?"

"I swear on every one of Marc's stitches that it's true. Not a drop of milk in the whole house."

"Marc's stitches — hmm. Interesting that Jessica hasn't mentioned any of *this*. You'd better tell me."

So I gave him the whole story, thinking, *You only think Jessica's in hot water, you poor bastard.* She must not have reached him last night. He had no idea the storm was about to break over his head.

"Uh-huh." I'd assume he was taking notes, only Nick never wrote anything down. Not like the cops on TV, that was for sure. "Uh-hmm. And you don't know where they are?"

"Not yet, but Sinclair and Tina are doing hours of drudgery research to figure that out."

"And Marc's at the General?" he asked, using the slang we used for the local hospital.

"Yeah, but he'll get out today. They ended up keeping him for a couple of nights, but not because anything wrong popped up. I think it was probably because he's big-time popular on the staff. But we're moving him to The Grand Hotel tonight."

"Where he'll stay indefinitely."

"Yeah, and the thing is, Jessica won't go. I

mean, flat-out refuses."

"Yeah?"

"Yeah. Sic her!"

"Doesn't she have, I don't know, a fucking Swiss chalet or something? Some other property besides the mansion where she can stay?"

"No, she doesn't care for Europe unless it's Tuscany, but surely you've got a chalet up your sleeve, John Deere Boy."

"Well, she doesn't have to stay there," he said grimly. "Not in Vampire Central."

"Yeah, so sock it to her." I didn't mention that Jessica wasn't staying at the mansion because she had nowhere else to go. He knew why she was staying, too, but didn't want to admit it, at least out loud. "Go tell her who's boss, by God."

"Oh, shut up," he said, and clicked off his phone.

CHAPTER 26

My semi-good deed done for the day, I rolled over, thumbed off my phone, dropped it on the bedside table (Sinclair was already bitching about the marks my phone and keys were leaving on various antiques around the house), and examined my feet.

There were advantages to being a vampire. I had refused to admit that for a long time and, even now, wasn't very happy when forced to make such an admission. The strength thing, and the speed. The hearing, of course.

More than once I'd been grateful for all three, usually while some psycho was trying to kill me. (Although if I hadn't been undead in the first place, said psycho would not have been trying to kill me, but screw it.)

And, although there were far more drawbacks than advantages to being queen, that had its high points, too.

But there were plenty of disads to being dead. One of the many was, you couldn't change your looks. I mean, you could, but whatever you did — paint your fingernails, cut your hair, curl your eyelashes — was undone when you rose the next night. I had no idea why, just like I didn't know how we could walk around with a heart rate of seven, or how we didn't need to breathe more than a couple of times an hour.

Thus, I always — *always* — needed a pedicure. (Thank God I had died only a few days after a cut and highlights!) It was depressing and a fact of life (or death, if you will), but there it was.

No time to mope. (Well. There was always time to mope. But I wasn't in the mood tonight.) I decided to do a quick one, myself, and twenty minutes later I was admiring my pink, newly smooth feet, and the wiggling toes with their coat of "Bitterness," which was actually a lovely soft gray.

Energized with the gorgeousness of my feet, I darted into the bathroom, rummaged around in the counter under the sink, and extracted a box of Crimson Tide, a wash-in/wash-out hair color. Stayed in for up to twelve shampoos. If you were alive, anyway.

When I got out of the shower, I couldn't help grinning at myself in the mirror. My hair was a dark, unnatural red; the shade made my skin paler than usual and my eyes seem green (they tended to fluctuate between blue and green, depending on what I was wearing and the quality of the light). And the box only cost twelve bucks. Since I'd be blond again tomorrow night, it wasn't worth going to the salon and dropping a hundred bucks for a custom dye job.

I dried off and got dressed, then opened my bedroom door, briefly wondered where my husband was (Sinclair only had to rest on occasion and, likely after sex, had waited until I conked out and then gone to the library or the fax machine or the local Kinko's to make color copies of something — wait, he had Tina to do that), furtively checked for unwanted ghosts, then bounded down the steps.

I could hear the fight long before I got to the kitchen door.

CHAPTER 27

"I can't believe you're staying! You *know,* and you're fucking *staying!*"

"Well, what about you, white boy?" Hmm. Jessica must be mega-pissed . . . "white boy" and "white girl" tended to come out only when she was furious, or scared. "You somehow forgot to mention that you're using my best friend to help you look good for the chief."

Wait. What?

"Not to mention, you expect her to take bullets for you if things get nasty. Slip your mind?"

"I'm not taking bullets for anyone," I announced, pushing open the door, "unless it's Beverly Feldman."

"Stay out of this, Betsy."

"Yeah, fuck off, blondie."

Sinclair's head came up with a jerk (he'd been seated at the counter, pretending to read the *Journal*), and he opened his mouth to hiss or roar something, but I overrode him with a breezy, "And a verrrrrry pleasant good evening to all of you, too."

The pleasantness of my greeting appeared to take the wind out of everyone's sails, not just his. I poured myself half the pitcher of orange juice and sat my ass down just like I belonged there.

It could be tricky, busting in on a fight. There was the "oh my God, I'm so sorry you didn't see me, I'll just scuttle back out the way I came" method, always popular with roommates of the female persuasion.

And there was my "hey, you're doing this in a public place — sort of, our kitchen — and you're fighting about me, so guess what? I'm staying" method, which I normally didn't have the nerve to try.

Jessica was eyeballing my head. "Nice hair."

"Thanks."

"It's very," Sinclair said carefully, "bright."

"Felt like a change."

"Mmmm. Detective Berry," Sinclair tried again, in a much calmer tone, but no less frightening, if you knew him, which we all did, "please do not speak to my wife that way in her own home."

"It's my girlfriend's home," Nick said, sounding sulky, but at least he was quieting down, too.

"Yes, so you delight in reminding me, and as I said earlier, I would be delighted to purchase the place from her at a fair market price. She could then move in with you, or not, as she liked, and as you liked, and several of your so-called problems would be over."

Nick had nothing to say to that, of course, and why would he? Sinclair was only telling the truth. In fact, I could see on Nick's face how very, very badly he wanted that option for Jessica.

Too bad he'd have about as much luck making her do anything she didn't want as I'd had in the past. Put it this way: I'd had more luck persuading the Ant not to wear so much polyester.

In fact, the only way he could maybe get her to leave would be if she moved —

Abruptly, Nick was on one knee. This startled Jessica, who kept her finger pointed at the space where his chest had been two seconds earlier. "I don't like you talking like — what the hell are you doing?"

He looked up at her soulfully, grabbed the hand that wasn't stabbing the air above him, and clutched it to his chest. "Jessica, will you marry me?"

"What?"

"Or at least move in with me? Right now?"

"*Très* romantic," Sinclair muttered, and I winked at him. I noticed his green teacup was empty, rose, and poured him a fresh cup, ignoring his raised eyebrows. It was possible I had never done such a thing before. Damn, I was in a good mood tonight! It could only mean doom was on the way. Doom, or the Ant.

"How sweet of you to ask." She yanked her hand out of Nick's no doubt sweaty grip. "And I'm only being half sarcastic when I say that, because you *do* think you're protecting me. But what a rotten way to begin living together or being engaged — so you can move me out of my best friend's house."

"It's your house!"

"That's true," I said, guzzling more juice. "It is."

"And you," he said, rounding on me. Definitely should have stayed out of this one. "Jessica's in mortal fucking danger — again! And this one is one hundred percent at your door, Oh Great Queen of the Suckheads!"

"You quit it," Jessica ordered, as the three of us pretended he wasn't one hundred percent right. "You were chortling over the possibility of the Fiends eating my friend —

136

except if those things take out Sinclair and Betsy —"

"Actually," I said, "we prefer 'Betsy and Sinclair.' "

"We certainly do not."

"— just what do you think they'll do to the rest of us?"

"Force us to buy time-shares in Cabo San Lucas," Tina suggested in a low voice, passing the local newspapers to Sinclair. I stifled a snicker.

"If they take out Sinclair and Betsy, who's gonna be safe?" Jessica asked. "Don't you get it, white boy? Half the time, those two walking wood ticks are the only thing between us and the *real* monsters."

"That was wonderful," Tina said, scuttling in with her head down, as if Nick and Jess were throwing frying pans in addition to words, "except for walking wood ticks. Good morning, Majesties. Good morning, Detective. Jessica."

They ignored her. Nick was still on his knees, but at least Jessica had stopped pointing at air. "Yeah, but you have to admit, most of the stuff they 'save' us from wouldn't be threatening us if not for *them* in the first place."

Oooh, ouch, good one. I certainly had no comeback.

"Yeah, well, with rank comes responsibility. Or is it with great power comes — anyway, that's what happens when you decide to shack up with dead monarchs, or even just a friend, something I knew long before Betsy and I were shacking up *here,* my come-lately lover." That was as close, normally, as Jess would come to "good point, you're right." "I remind you that she's been on the scene a lot longer than you have."

"You think I don't know that?"

"And that I *wouldn't* be on the scene if it hadn't been for her," she continued quietly. "I'd be a month dead by now. But she saved my life. Better: my appendix grew back, and so did my tonsils, and I've never felt better."

"Say *what?*" I asked, choking on my juice. Tina had frozen in the act of handing several faxes to Sinclair. And he just looked at me with those dark, expressionless eyes and said nothing. "Stuff that got cut out of you grew back?"

"Of course I'm grateful to her, she's alive, isn't she?" he snapped. "She's walking around not arrested, right? I didn't mention her secret to any of the thirty-some *Pioneer Press* reporters I know. Did I?"

"Yikes. Thanks." Reporters? Arrested?

Man, I was getting an awful lot of new information to process at once. Time for more juice.

"You haven't done any of those things, because you don't want me to *dump* your sorry ass, not out of gratitude to Betsy."

Oh, and the quarterback scores!

Nick slowly got up off the floor, brushed off his knees, and turned to me. "You know this is your fault."

"I do know. I'm sorry, Nick. I tried to make her leave."

"I can make her leave," Sinclair said pleasantly, watching Nick.

"No, no," I said, pouring the rest of the pitcher into my glass and draining it in three gulps. Other liquids didn't kill the thirst for blood — nothing but, well, *blood* could do that — but they helped a little. The household was used to watching me go through a gallon of juice at breakfast. Though breakfast tended to be at ten o'clock at night these days. "Nobody's gonna make Jessica do anything, I think we got that established in the seventh grade. And Nick's right. The Fiends thing — it's my fault. I just — I just sort of forgot about them for a while."

"Typical," Guess Who sneered.

I could feel my good mood draining away, sort of like the OJ out of the pitcher.

139

Because I made this mess, I made it happen — or allowed, through inaction, it to happen. I felt shitty about it, but it was way beyond late for that. Feeling shitty wasn't going to solve the problem. Probably more people dying would, and I absolutely hated that.

The really awful thing was, the thought of the deaths to come didn't depress me so much as it made me tired.

CHAPTER 28

"Officer, I would like to report a crime. Several crimes."

Ah, the perfect touch to destroy the last of my good mood. I sighed and rested my forehead on the counter. "He's a detective, you dimwit; note the plain clothes and the holster. And he can't hear you."

"What?" Nick said.

"Never mind that," the Ant snapped. She was standing in the middle of the stove. *That* was surprising. Usually the ghosts behaved like they were still alive and tried not to walk through things unless they absolutely had to — say, through a door that was shut (because, natch, they couldn't grasp the knob). The center burners came up to the bottom button on her too-tight lime green blouse. It clashed awfully with her bright yellow hair and made her skin look positively greenish. "Tell him about how you're keeping me prisoner."

My head snapped up so quickly I nearly overturned my chair. "I am not! You're here of your own free will, Antonia, and the sooner you figure that out the happier I'll be."

"Make that all of us," Jessica added. "Get lost, Mrs. Taylor."

"You should tell the help not to speak to me," she said triumphantly, thrilled that someone else was acknowledging her presence.

"You know damned well that's Jessica!"

"Is that bigoted bitch slamming me from beyond the grave? Where is she?"

"What difference does it make?" I sighed. "You can't touch her."

"No, but I can throw things through her. Make me feel better, anyway." She darted to one of the tables, snatched up a plate, and hurled it toward the fridge. Where it fluttered to the ground, since, to save on dish washing, we tended to use paper plates for breakfast.

"Stop that, and she's in the *stove,* okay? The stove!"

"What the fuck is going on?"

"Betsy's dead stepmother is haunting her," Jessica told him.

"Oh, that's —" Nick threw his hands up in the air and walked around in a tight little circle.

"The last straw?" Sinclair suggested. "I quite agree. So snatch up your girlfriend and flee for your lives."

"That's it," Jessica said. "I just doubled your rent."

"Everything in the whole world sucks." I rested my chin in my hand and stared past Sinclair's shoulder at the window over the sink. "Every. Single. Thing."

"A pity," Sinclair replied. "And you were in such a charming mood, too. Although a little warning would be appreciated the next time you do something drastic to your hair."

"Oh, it'll be blond again tomorrow, who cares? What was I thinking, when I said I could do this job? I must have been out of my mind!"

"That's the spirit," Nick said, instantly cheering up.

"Stop that," Sinclair and Jessica ordered in unison. They looked at each other in surprise, almost laughed, and then Jessica continued. "You're doing the best you can. Nobody expects more."

"Ha!" I pointed to her boyfriend. "He does."

"And I can't be the only one," Nick added.

"Well, what's she supposed to do, smart guy? By all means, enlighten all of us. How would *you* help run the vampire kingdom?"

"I'd start," he replied sweetly, "by rounding up all my 'subjects' and blowing their faces off."

Sinclair snorted. "Then let us say, for the sake of argument, that you were the king, and you did that. I'm sure you can see the consequences."

I could feel the confidence I'd gained after defeating Marjorie draining out of me. Whatever I'd done to Marjorie had been, like most of the great events of my life/death, both a fluke and dumb luck. I was lucky to be alive (ahem), and it was nuts to read any more into it than that.

"I'm guessing I can't abdicate," I said to Tina.

She looked more than a little taken aback. "Ah . . . no."

"That's quite enough," my husband said coolly. "You've let this silly little man rattle you and for no good reason."

"Yeah, but the Fiend thing really is my fault."

"And none of mine?"

"Hey, yeah!" Nick said. "It's *both* your faults!"

Sinclair ignored him. "I knew, as you did, that they were out there in Minnetonka. I chose, as you did, to do nothing."

"Yeah, but if I'd done like you wanted, they'd all be dead, and we wouldn't be in this mess."

"And if wishes were horses, beggars would ride."

"What?"

"An old saying of my mother's."

"Very old," Tina said, almost — but not quite! — smiling.

"Elizabeth, it's far too late to play the 'what if' game. We have a situation. We are dealing with it. The opinions of the occasional passing human are of no import. I am the king, you are the queen, so shall it be forever."

"Or, at least," Jessica added, "for a thousand years."

"Passing human?" Nick asked.

"I noticed you put yourself first." I slid my empty glass over to him. "Pour me something, will you? Something. Anything."

"Why don't you snack on Detective Berry?" Tina suggested. "That would make us all feel better."

"You assholes stay away from me," Nick warned, backing up until his butt hit the kitchen door.

"Then do not," my husband said, "let us keep you."

CHAPTER 29

"Well, that was —"

"Can you believe the nerve of that guy?" Jessica bitched, plunking down in the chair opposite Sinclair. "Asking me to marry him just so I'd move."

"Perhaps it was the right question under the wrong circumstances," Sinclair suggested, which I thought was an elegant way of looking at it.

"And perhaps he's losing his damn mind."

"There is always that," he admitted.

"Are we all going to pretend that he didn't make some really good points?" I demanded.

"Oh, right," Jess replied. "I forgot: this is all about *you.*"

"Well, it kind of is," I grumbled, chastened.

"When you are older," my husband said, folding up his newspaper (I don't know *why* he didn't read them online), "you will see the futility of second-guessing yourself and wasting time with it."

"Great. I can't fucking wait. Hey, when I'm older, do you think I'll turn into an emotionless robot like someone we all —"

"Betsy!" The kitchen door swung open, and Nick stuck his head inside. "There's a vampire here to see you. I think she's a vampire. She fucking stinks, man."

"Great. A new subject to disappoint! Let's go see her, so I can let her down right away."

"Can someone let me off of the pity train now?" Jessica asked, getting up and following me. "This is my stop."

I thought I heard Sinclair snicker, but when I glanced at him, he was as smooth-faced as usual. And, thank God, the Ant wasn't following us. Perhaps she'd popped out again. I'd hope it was permanent, except I wasn't *that* dumb.

"Thank you, Detective Berry, you would make a fine butler. Now run along."

"Like I want to stay?" he retorted, falling into step beside us. I wondered who the new vamp was. Maybe a straggler of sorts who had just heard about the new king and queen. Now and again a vampire from the middle of nowhere would show up to pay tribute (gag). "Besides, I gotta get back to work."

"He did," I whispered to Jessica, "get here really quick. He must have hung up and rushed right over. That's pretty sweet, doncha think?"

"Hey, that's right! *You* called him and told him about the Fiends!"

Oh, shit.

Jessica was shaking her head. "The things I'm gonna do to you when we have a little privacy — I think it's time to pour vinegar on your Jimmy Choos again."

"No!" I practically screamed, beyond horrified. "Once was enough!"

"Obviously not, since I've done it twice."

I'd probably put up a psychological block the size of the Great Wall.

"Anyway, here she is," Nick was saying. "I put her in the, uh, other parlor." He meant the one that was the least presentable of the four we had. Or was it five? Anyway, the wallpaper was faded and even torn in some places; the rugs were worn. And it smelled musty, like old books in an attic. We hardly ever spent any time in there. In a mansion this size, it was no trouble to ignore the less comfortable rooms and stick with the ones you liked. "She, uh, really stinks pretty bad."

"Maybe she got caught out late and had to pop into the sewer," Tina suggested. "That's happened to me a time or two."

"I'll see you later," Nick said, giving Jessica a noisy smack on the lips.

"To be continued," she warned him, but at least she kissed him back.

"Hello," Sinclair said. "I am King Sinclair, and this is Queen Elizabeth."

The vampire, who had been huddled by the fireplace, turned to face us. "I know who you both are."

Tina took one look, shrieked, "Clara the Fiend!" and launched herself at the smaller, smellier vampire.

CHAPTER 30

Which was unbelievably startling, to say the least. Before I could move, or think, or react in any way, Sinclair's hand shot out almost faster than I could track, and he caught Tina by the back of her sweater. He held her in midair, her short legs kicking back and forth.

Clara the Fiend had backed into the nearest corner and was pressing herself into it as if she could shove herself through the wall and disappear. Given Tina's sudden viciousness, I could hardly blame her. "Please, I came alone! Please, I just want to talk!"

"Eric, put me *down.*" Tina was practically spitting. And she'd used his first name . . . oooh, he was in trouble now. "Put me down right now so I can — and you! You get out of my master's house, you wretch! You pathetic creeping *thing,* you disgust us all, and you insult their majesties with your very presence! How dare you come to their home! Get out, before I kill you!"

"Tina, it's okay —" Jessica started.

"Oh, Jesus." Nick had his gun out and was standing in front of Jessica. The gun barrel kept wavering between Clara and Tina.

I couldn't blame him. I'd never seen Tina so out-of-control furious. I mean, *I* was scared of her, and I knew that under ninety-nine-point-nine percent of the circumstances, she not only wouldn't hurt me, she'd give her life to save me. Even Sinclair, much bigger and stronger, had to hang on to her with both hands. "Jesus, Jesus, these are the guys that clocked me in the nose the other day. These are the Fiends?"

"They are," Sinclair replied, turning pale at the reference to God's son. "Tina, calm yourself. She appears to have come in peace."

"And she'll leave in pieces!"

"Good one," Jessica piped up from behind Nick, "if a bit clichéd."

"Out, out *now,* you vile bitch! You *get out of our house!*"

"Holy shit," Jessica muttered. "I have no idea which one to be more scared of."

"Makes two of us," I whispered back. Maybe somebody should slap her? It always worked in the movies. And after you clocked

151

them, they always said, "Thanks, I needed that."

I didn't really see Tina saying anything of the sort, so I reached up — Sinclair had hoisted Tina pretty high — and grabbed a flailing fist. "Tina, relax. If Clara tries anything, you can kill her all over the place."

The mad frenetic kicking stopped. "You swear it? Swear it on your crown," she ordered, then instantly changed her mind. "No: swear it on the king."

"I swear on my husband's testicles that if Clara tries even one sneaky thing, you can play soccer with her head."

Tina abruptly stopped struggling. Sinclair, just as abruptly, set her down. He didn't seem particularly concerned for his genitals, despite my promise. Maybe he thought this would all end up okay. I sure as hell didn't know that for sure.

CHAPTER 31

"All right," he said to the huddled, smelly vampire. (Nick was right: she reeked.) "Suppose you tell us why you're here, Clara."

"That's not my name," she said. "My name is Stephanie Connor. Thank you for seeing me, dread king."

I heard a commotion and turned to see Nick trying to haul a very reluctant Jessica out of the room. She kept yanking her hand out of his and hissing at him to hush up, she wanted to hear.

"Detective Berry, perhaps you could escort Jessica somewhere safer?" Sinclair asked, soooo politely, so I knew he was really sticking the knife in. "Anywhere outside of Ramsey County would be preferable."

"Dread king, may I — ?"

"Nick, let me *go*."

"It's a little chaotic right now," I told Cl— uh, Stephanie. "Give us a minute." I turned to Jess. "You know I'll tell you all about it later. Why don't you am-scray for now?"

Giving me an "I'll deal with you later" glare, Jessica allowed herself to be herded out. Nick shot me a look, too, one I found startling: pure gratitude.

Tina was panting and patting her hair back into place. Thank goodness she'd worn a ponytail. I hated to think of the masses of blond hair flying all over the place. "Would you," she managed through gritted teeth, "like a refreshment?"

Cl— uh, Stephanie looked shocked, like it was a trap. The trap of the Coca-Cola products. Ah, I'd fallen into that sweet, sweet trap a time or two myself. "Uh, no. No thank you, ma'am."

"My name is Tina." Still forcing the words out through teeth ground so tightly, I could hear them rasping against each other. "I am the adjutant to their majesties."

Adj-u-*what?* Was that, like, a super secretary or something? I was pretty sure I'd never heard that word out loud before. Maybe I'd read it, but it was spelled completely differently. I made a mental note to ask about it later. Sinclair would know. He knew pretty much everything.

"Why don't you come out of the corner,"

I said, crossing the room and offering my hand, "and have a seat? Oh, and unless this is a trap, thanks for coming out to see us all peacefully and stuff."

Sinclair had stiffened when I'd moved toward Stephanie, but relaxed when all she did was meekly follow me and look down at one of the couches. "I'm . . . dirty. I'll stand, if that won't, um, offend." Another nervous glance at Tina, who was examining the rips in her sweater. I tried, and failed, not to raise my eyebrows: she'd been struggling so hard to get away from Sinclair she'd torn the seams out from under both arms. And wool was *tough.* Cripes.

"No, please, take a seat. A little dirt won't kill anyone." Oh, shit, I said kill. Reminding her of what the Fiends had tried to do to us. "Um, I mean hurt anyone." Oh, shit! "Um, just sit the hell down, okay?"

She sat on the far, far edge, looking like she wanted to leap away at any second. And I could see why she smelled — her clothes were filthy, and the mingled odor of dirt, dog poop, and blood came off her.

I wondered where they were sleeping during the day. They had no money or resources unless they killed or robbed or both.

In the past, when a vampire came back to him- or herself, they could go to the library in Minneapolis and find out who they were, if they owned property, if they still had a bank account . . . like that. And Marjorie, the dead betrayer, would give them a hand. It occurred to me that we needed a new system in place . . . like two months ago. Because right now, a vampire who wasn't an out of control newborn had few options. Just feed and hide, feed and hide.

While you live in luxury on Summit Avenue.

I shoved that thought away, hard.

"Now," Sinclair was saying, "what brings you to us, Ms. Connor?"

She picked at the knees of her torn, stained jeans. "I, uh, thought maybe we could talk." She had a mild southern accent — Virginia, maybe? Missouri? Not a drawl, but almost. Of course, anyone who sounded like they weren't from the set of *Fargo* or *Drop Dead Gorgeous* sounded southern or eastern to me. "About our, um, problem."

"Do you represent the interest of your companions, or only your own?"

She blinked at that one, then seemed to decode it in her mind. "Oh. Um, I'm here by myself. I mean, the others don't know I've come."

I listened hard for the sounds of ambush, but could only hear the usual household noise. Then I yowled as the furnace kicked on, which sounded at the moment like a jet plane taking off from inside my skull.

Startled, everyone twitched or looked in my direction. "Sorry," I said. "I just remembered that *30 Rock* is a rerun this week."

Stephanie looked more confused than before, but that was all right. I noticed neither Sinclair nor Tina took a seat, so I did — straight across from our visitor. "You came by yourself," I said, "that seems pretty obvious now. Sorry about Tina jumping on you like that. She had a flashback to the Civil War." I ignored Sinclair's snort. "So what's on your mind?"

"And why should we think anything you say is the truth?"

I shot a look at Sinclair — that sounded a little too much like Nick to suit me.

"I don't — I can't *prove* I'm telling the truth," she said, a little desperately. "I guess the others could be parked a mile away, and this is step one in some elaborate, I dunno, plan? But it's not. We're — we're not well organized."

"You looked pretty organized when you hurt our friends," I said mildly. "They had to go to the hospital." A minor exaggeration — once Nick's nosebleed had cleared up, he'd been fine. It was a measure of his contempt for our lifestyle that he hadn't

157

thought twice about strange vampires punching him in the face and then attacking us. It was only when I'd given him the gory Fiend details that he had realized exactly what had happened — and what it meant for Jessica. "We were pretty bummed about that."

"Well. The others are — they're mad at you."

"But not you," Sinclair said, soooo silkily.

"I am. I mean, I was. How could you — I dunno." She had an interesting way of speaking . . . not slowly, exactly, and maybe it was the accent. But it was almost like she was searching for each word and found it almost every time, in the unused corners of her mind. I reminded myself that last week she'd been batshit crazy. No idea who she was, where she was, what she was.

"Did you guys sort of 'wake up' all at once, then?"

Stephanie looked, if possible, even more uncomfortable. Clearly not a subject she wanted to discuss. Too bad.

"Well, each time Garrett came we felt — I dunno, better? We felt *more.* And then, a few days ago, it was like — like I'd been asleep for a long time, only now, right now I *knew,* I remembered I was Stephanie. I don't . . ." She shook her head. "I don't know who killed me. And I couldn't tell you where I grew up, or the name of my first boyfriend, or even where I went to middle school. I remember some things — my first job out of high school, and the name of the man I almost married, but — mostly I remember the blood. Drinking all of that . . . that dead blood. For years and years and years." She cleared her throat and worked her jaws like she wanted to spit, but didn't dare.

I glanced at Sinclair and Tina, then took the plunge. "The thing is, Stephanie, it was kind of our only option."

"Once we took killing you off the table," Sinclair said pleasantly.

"I didn't want to kill you guys, but I couldn't set you free, either."

"Why?"

"Oh, boy." I thought about the best way to explain this. "Stephanie, you have no idea how scary you guys were." Was *scary* the right word? I probably shouldn't have told her that. Fuck it. "The few times you got out, you ripped people just to *pieces.* There was no way we could let you have live blood. You would have killed the donor every time."

"Oh. Yes, I see that now." Except she sounded like she didn't, not exactly. "I

159

should go now."

"You don't believe me," I said.

Her eyes betrayed her emotion: trapped. I had seen through her lie, and now all she could imagine was that she was in fantastic trouble.

"Stephanie, I'm not saying I've treated you and the others perfectly. I think I had the right idea when I began to feed Garrett, regardless of the danger. And I think Garrett had the right idea, when he began to feed all of you. I'm glad —"

"Glad?!"

"Yes, glad, Tina, that he did so. And I hope you and the others can forgive me, and see that I really did start the awakening for all of you. Just not fast enough, or well enough. I can do better, if you give me the chance."

I warned Sinclair, with a look, from saying a word. Stephanie was plainly trying to digest what I had told her. For all I knew, she was still trying to understand some of the words. Or maybe she had one of those 1970s game shows playing in a loop in her mind ("Things you kill. Things you maim. Things you wish you could drink instead of blood! YES, YOU'VE WON THE *$64,000 PYRAMID!*").

"Thank you, Your Majesty," she finally

said. "I have to get back. The others will miss me. They'd kill me if they knew I was here."

"Then why *are* you here?" Tina asked.

"To find out more. To learn if what the others say is true."

"What do the others say?"

"That we are the queen's wolves, bred for her wars, and the foreshadow of what the world will become under her reign."

We all took that in for a moment. It was so horrible, so preposterous . . . I didn't know whether to laugh or cry.

"Perhaps you could educate your colleagues," Sinclair suggested, "as to the true nature of this queen."

"Well, I would try to talk to them, but it wouldn't work." Stephanie shrugged. "And I couldn't try too hard, or they might kill *me.*"

I was trying not to gape at her, and failing. In my efforts to apologize and see her point of view, I had missed how fearful she still was . . . and how undependable an ally she would be.

"You have overstayed your welcome," Sinclair said, which felt a bit harsh to me, but I had no idea how to correct him.

"All right, but . . ." She licked her lips. "I am afraid we will come back soon."

161

"Not if you obey your queen," Tina pointed out.

"I cannot stop them."

"If you cannot stop them," Sinclair pointed out, "then you cannot help us. And if you cannot help us, we cannot let you go back."

I stared at Sinclair, trying to see where this logic train was going to end. *Nowhere happy,* I told myself.

"We cannot let you stay here, any more easily than we can let you go back. The effort to watch over you securely, combined with the potential costs if we fail, lead to only one solution. Tina," he ended calmly, "kill her."

CHAPTER 32

"No no no no no no *no!*" Only just in time did I leap from my seat and jump in front of the cringing Stephanie, who had shoved herself so far back she had nearly disappeared into the couch.

Tina slammed into me hard enough to make me stagger — she'd launched herself the moment Sinclair got "kill" out of his mouth. Like she'd been ready the whole time. Like she was waiting for it.

"Bad, Tina! Down!"

"Elizabeth, do not —"

"Keep her away from me!" Stephanie squealed, scrambling off the couch.

I managed to grab Tina by the shoulders and hold her at arm's length. At least she wasn't trying to kick me. "You guys, you guys! We are not killing her, she came in peace, and she's leaving the same way."

"Like hell," Tina managed through gritted teeth.

"Don't listen to her! You can go. Good-bye, Stephanie. I'm sorry about what happened to you."

"Do not," Tina snarled, "apologize. To that thing."

Meanwhile Stephanie was halfway out the door. "Thankyouforseeingmegoodbye."

I let go of Tina, and we all listened to the rapidly retreating footfalls.

"Soft," was my husband's verdict. "Much too soft. Even now. Hmm."

"And you're too hard," I shot back with my own judgment. That's right — two could play the judge-and-jury game! "And too stupid. And don't be siccing Tina on people, like she's your own personal pit bull!"

"But I am," she replied at the exact moment Sinclair said, "But she is."

" 'Kill her,' my God! Haven't you ever heard of a flag of truce? These Fiends are growing. Maybe they can grow emotions beyond hate and fear. Maybe they can become . . . like Garrett. Like us. Why is that so hard for you two to see?"

They'd flinched when I'd broken the commandment, but now they were both giving me that *look*.

"There will come a time when you will regret having let her leave," my bloodthirsty psycho husband said.

Tina was shaking her head. "You should have let me kill her, Majesty. If for no other reason than the audacity she showed in coming here, soliciting an apology, and giving nothing in return! Not even an offer to *try* to lift a finger to stop the others."

"She'll remember I was nice to her."

"Mercy," Sinclair lectured, "is a poor weapon."

I stared at him. Sometimes — many times — I didn't know him. At all. "It's the only one I'm using right now."

"*You* don't have to use a weapon at all," Tina pointed out. "I would take care of these problems for you."

I think what finally made me snap was seeing Tina degrade herself — describe herself as nothing but a deadly vessel, when I knew she was so much more. Or maybe I was just pissed at my fucking arrogant husband.

"The only problem I have," I hissed, "is a couple of subjects who don't think I have what it takes to be queen! Perhaps if they'd sit down, shut up, and listen to her, they'd learn something!"

Yuck, did I just refer to myself in the third person? Even weirder, Tina looked embarrassed beyond belief, and quickly sat down. Sinclair also sat down, much more slowly, with an odd expression on his face — a cross between outrage and pride.

Well. Now what?

"So." I started to pace. "Let's figure this out. Where are the Fiends staying during the day?"

"I would be more interested in how and where they are feeding," Sinclair said. "I would ask Detective Berry to look for any unusual homicides, but he is not our friend at the moment. His loyalty is solely with Jessica. Perhaps another source can help us."

"He'd look for vampire attacks in two seconds, regardless of how he feels about you, me, and Tina."

I was about to elaborate, when the front door was slammed open and an all-too-familiar voice greeted us with, "What the *hell* is going on? I leave this shitheap for three days, and the fuckin' Fiends are loose, my boyfriend's practically catatonic, and the smelliest bitch I've ever fuckin' seen practically ran me down on the porch! Not to mention I nearly got into a fender bender with the devil who looks like Miss Fuckin' February! Jesus fucking Christ, what the hell is going on?"

Antonia the werewolf was home.

"Oh, gosh, Antonia, you know you

shouldn't talk like that."

As well as the devil's daughter.

CHAPTER 33

Two ridiculously beautiful women hurried into the parlor, and I sighed. I often felt like the homely judge at a swimsuit competition; all the women in our house were just so pretty.

Antonia Wolfton, current werewolf and former psychic, was a lean, tall brunette (almost as tall as me), with striking dark eyes and the palest, softest skin I'd ever seen on someone alive. She was like a foul-mouthed milkmaid.

The waves of her hair crashed and bounced halfway down her back. Her lips were rosebud pink, and when her hair was pulled back by a red ribbon, as it was now, she looked like Snow White.

"I thought you were gonna get the fucking driveway fixed," she griped. "And what'd you do to my boy toy while I was gone, you rotten bitch?"

I didn't laugh — barely — but then, I was

used to it. For Antonia, that was a downright warm greeting. It was just so *weird,* those excellent good looks, that amazing figure, that perfect mouth . . . and then the *words* that kept coming out over and over again. It was as if God had fused a swimsuit model with a teamster.

"Oh, now, stop it," the devil's daughter (really!) said with gentle reproach. "The driveway's not that bad, and I'm sure Sinclair and Betsy have lots more important things on their minds." Laura Goodman (don't laugh) looked like, as Antonia had put it once, "a dirty old man's wet dream," with long, butterscotch blond hair, big blue eyes, and long strong limbs. Her nose was a sculpted delight, her mouth wide and generous.

She had never had a pimple.

I think I mentioned before that Laura had a unique way of rebelling against her mother. When your mother was the devil, *the* devil, there wasn't much you could do for rebellion; after all, how do you rebel against the embodiment of evil?

You go to church. You teach Sunday school. You volunteer for soup kitchens. You are kind to children and small animals. You constantly watch your language. You pray.

That's how.

"What are you guys doing here?"

"Ha!" Antonia brayed. "I knew you'd play dumb. Actually, you can't *not* play dumb, huh, Bets? My boyfriend called, and he's a gibbering wreck. Something about his 'foul behavior' and 'base betrayal' and how there can be no forgiveness 'n' shit, then I got bored, so I kind of tuned him out."

"And yet," Sinclair said dryly, "here you are."

"Shit, yeah. Apparently everything's going to hell around here. You dummies *need* me."

"You don't especially need me," Laura said, almost apologetically. "But I got worried when you canceled our lunch." From anyone else, that would have sounded reproachful. Laura was too tenderhearted to pull something like that, even though it hadn't been one lunch I'd blown off, it had been two. "I apologize for dropping by without calling, but I was beginning to worry."

There was a method to my madness, and I wasn't at all happy to see my sister here. Bottom line? I didn't want her anywhere near the Fiends, especially since we didn't know when they'd come calling again. Part of the reason they'd gotten better so quickly was because they had drunk a combination of my blood . . . and hers.

It wouldn't be understating the point to say I wished she'd leave the state until this was all straightened out. I was just too chickenshit to tell her.

"It's been really crazy around here," I managed.

" 'Really crazy'?" Antonia sneered. "Oh, okay. That's not the Betsy play-it-down machine getting into gear, is it?"

"My gosh," Tina said mildly, "what happened to your arm?"

"Oh. That." Antonia gleefully rolled up her sleeve and displayed her disgusting injury to all of us. What I hadn't noticed turned out to be a hideous blackish red bruise running from her wrist to past her elbow. "Jumped from one of the bluffs and miscalculated the distance."

"Antonia, you've got to take better care of yourself," I scolded. "You're not used to changing into a wolf, and besides, last night wasn't even the full moon . . . what are you doing jumping off bluffs?"

"Quickest way to get where I wanna go. Anyway, tomorrow night is the full moon, and then we'll have fun fun fun." She was positively gleeful, and I couldn't blame her.

"One of these days you'll miscalculate and break your rotten little neck."

This was true, despite Antonia's glare. See, when she first came to us, Antonia was a very special kind of werewolf. She was born into the pack, had a werewolf mom and dad, but had never changed. Never become a wolf during the full moon.

Instead, she could see the future. It wasn't always clear, and sometimes only after the fact could we figure out exactly what she'd been trying to warn us against. (Like most supernatural abilities, it sounded better on paper than the real deal.) But she was never wrong — just oblique.

Until Marjorie the librarian came along — in addition to giving me a cursed engagement ring and snatching my groom, she'd locked up Antonia as well — and Garrett. Do you have any idea how claustrophobic werewolves are? They dealt with enclosed spaces the way I did with knockoffs. Just a bad, bad situation all around.

Anyway, while I was busy killing Marjorie and soaking up all her evil energy, I let Antonia have a blast of it (most of the rest I saved to revive Sinclair and cure Jessica's cancer). It was the first time she had ever changed into a wolf, and she'd been enjoying it ever since.

As I said, she had lived her whole life among werewolves while being unable to change into a wolf herself. Now she saw herself as complete, and didn't seem to mind the loss of her psychic abilities as a trade-off.

But, as Laura pointed out, she was taking too many risks. Nothing we would say would talk her out of it, either; she thought she was invincible even when she wasn't in wolf form.

"So what'd you dimwits do to my boy toy?" she demanded, rolling down her sleeve. I noticed for the first time that she was wearing one of my oxford shirts, and stifled a groan. Antonia had the table manners of Boss Hog. Assuming I ever got the blouse back, I'd probably have to chuck it. "He's practically fetal with wretchedness."

"You could tell that over the phone?" Sinclair asked, amused.

"Enhanced senses," she sneered, staring him straight in the eye — the height of rudeness for a werewolf. "Way better than anything a dead guy can do."

"It's really none of my business," Laura said, fiddling with a lock of her hair and looking at the assembly of personalities in the room, "but something certainly seems to be going on. Are you all right?"

"As rain," I said heartily.

Antonia and Laura stared at me.

"Well." I coughed. "There have been a *few* things going on . . ."

CHAPTER 34

We ended up sitting down in the kitchen and telling the girls everything. If for no other reason than they had to be warned — Antonia lived there most of the time, after all, and Laura was famous for the pop-in.

Antonia's face got darker; Laura's became more concerned. When I finished (after frequent interruptions from the love of my life and his personal pit bull), there was a long silence, broken by Antonia bawling, "Garrett! Get your ass up here!"

"But you could have been killed!" Laura said, rubbing her ear as Antonia disappeared in the direction of the basement. "Why didn't you call me?"

"It would be unsafe to have you near such dangerous vampires at this time," Sinclair said bluntly.

"What? I could help," she said, hurt.

I glared at Subtle Boy. "Honey, it's not personal. It's just — the Fiends are like this because of my blood *and* your blood."

"But you're the one who made me —"

"I know, I know. Like I said, it's not personal. But I can't take a chance of one of them attacking you, getting a mouthful, and getting even more dangerous. And, no offense, sometimes your temper gets the better of you." To put it very freaking mildly.

"It does not!"

"Hon. It so totally does."

"That was one time!"

"Are you talking about the time you beat the shit out of Garrett, or the time you killed the serial killer?"

Laura's mouth thinned, but before she could reply, Garrett came skidding into the kitchen on his back, as if someone was using him to play shuffleboard. We heard footfalls, and then Antonia slapped the door open.

"It's one thing to want to help your comrades in arms," she told him as he climbed slowly to his feet. "But something else to put your friends in danger and then hide from what you've done. Literally hide — have you even been out of the basement since you called me?"

"No," Garrett said.

"And you're living under her roof! Calling for me to come save you, calling from *her* phone! You made this mess, Garrett, and much as I love you, you'll fix it, or I'll pull all your limbs off."

"It's not his fault." Sure, she'd been saying things I had secretly been thinking, but I could have cried at the expression on poor Garrett's face. He was trying to shake the long hair out of his face, and was too ashamed to look at any of us. "He didn't know what would happen. He's only been speaking English for two damn months!"

"It is my fault," he said dully, looking at the floor.

Antonia's tone gentled about a fraction, and she bent to help him to his feet. "I know we have different backgrounds — and the age thing — I'm not stupid, I *know* we're different. Shit, we're not even the same species; needless to say we weren't brought up the same way. But I can't be with someone who puts his friends in danger and then hides to save himself."

"The Fiends are my responsibility and no one else's," I said, resisting the urge to step between Antonia and Garrett. "This isn't a debate we're having, okay? The Fiends are my problem. How they got on the radar is irrelevant. Does everyone understand that?"

This, as I knew it would, put Antonia in a major bind. A creature of pack leaders and strict hierarchies, when she was under this roof, I was her pack leader pro tem. She could tease me, mouth off, borrow my clothes without asking (though she knew better than to touch my shoes), and give me untold rations of shit, but it was very, very difficult for her to out-and-out cross me.

In a strange way I knew I could count on Antonia's obedience and support more than anyone else's in the room. Of course, I had no power over the devil's daughter, except her willingness to please a sister.

Tina obeyed me in superficial matters (while you're up could you get me a glass of orange juice? Could you show Officer Berry the door? Could you hit Sinclair over the head with the fax machine?), but on matters like this, her allegiance was clearly to Sinclair.

I had zero power over Sinclair.

"If you're taking responsibility, I guess it's none of my business," Antonia said with a shrug. "But holler next time one of them comes calling. Might be fun. As for you . . ." She pointed to Garrett, and he followed her, slump-shouldered, toward the basement door.

"I hope she isn't too hard on him," Laura worried.

"Ha," I said sourly. Already I could hear things crashing. "She'll be hard on him. But at least they'll kiss and make up."

"You think?"

"Who else could stand to be with either one of them?"

"Point," my sister conceded, and we both laughed.

I asked after BabyJon, whom Laura had been watching, before dropping him off at my mother's for the day.

"She'll be underwhelmed," she pointed out diplomatically, when I suggested Baby-Jon might need to stay there longer.

"Laura, I know she thought her baby-rearing days were long over —"

"And don't forget BabyJon is a constant reminder of her late ex-husband's infidelity."

"— and I respect that. But she still loves BabyJon, kind of, and she won't want him harmed. If we laid it out for her, told her he could either stay here and maybe get nibbled by Fiends, or stay with her and spit up on her Civil War bullet collection, you know which one she'd pick. But please don't tell her why BabyJon needs to stay. She'll just worry."

"I'll come up with something," Laura promised at once. God, she was so low maintenance. When she wasn't in the grip of a simmering, murderous rage. "It wouldn't be such a big deal, but I think your mother is still taking your father's death kind of hard. Harder than — I mean, hard."

Laura had corrected herself because she'd been about to say "harder than you," which was nothing but the truth. I'd been fairly indifferent about my dad in life and wasn't sure how I felt about him dying. It was even partly my *fault* he was dead and I wasn't sure how I felt.

When *I* had died and come back as a vampire, he'd essentially told me to stay away. Seemed only fair that I return the favor . . . to seem like I didn't care if he was gone forever. But then, that sounded so cold and mean, I couldn't stand it. He was my *father.*

"Which reminds me," I sighed, slumping in my seat, "you won't even guess who's been hanging around."

"Umm . . . Detective Berry?"

"Well, yeah, but also my stepmother . . . and your birth mother."

Laura had been polishing an apple on her immaculate buttercup yellow wool blazer, but stopped. "She's haunting you?"

"Yeppers."

"What does she need you to do?"

"That's the super fun part. She won't tell me."

Laura shook her head; gorgeous blond strands flew about her face and then settled perfectly. "That does it. I can no longer stay away from your house for more than a week. I miss too much!"

"It's not always like this," I sighed.

"In fact, I'm going to stick to you like cow poop on a Furragrammo."

"It's Fair-uh-gahm-oh . . . and don't even say it!" I begged, but it turned out she wasn't exaggerating.

CHAPTER 35

"I still don't understand why Midwestern Barbie is along for the ride," Detective Nick whined as we pulled onto the highway.

"One of the three of us in this horrid little car has my sister's best interests at heart. One of them isn't you," Laura said sweetly, "and the other isn't her."

I forced a cough. "Any luck with that, um, errand Jessica asked you to run?" After some discussion, Tina, Sinclair, and I had agreed Jessica was the best person to ask Nick to keep an eye out for unusual murders.

"You mean have your runaway pets mangled any citizens? Not that we can tell. Yet. And again, if I didn't make this clear: nice one, doorknob."

"I *said* I was sorry," I grumped, slumping against the backseat. (Yes, he'd dumped me in the back — at least it was a plain car and not a cruiser.)

"You stop picking on her," Laura ordered. "She's doing the best she can. Although when she shuts out family members it only makes things —"

"I'm sitting right behind you. I can, sorry to say, hear everything. Where are we going, anyway?"

"Got a tip that our bad guys might be meeting down here."

"Wait, 'bad guys' the Fiends? Or —"

"No, my bad guys, dummy. I hate to break this to you for the twentieth time, but it's not always about you, Betsy."

I disagreed, but let it pass. "And a fellow cop showing up isn't going to scare the alleged bad guys away?"

"We think they're actually contracting out — giving the info to one of their perps, a guy (or gal) they can count on to pull the trigger. Do a few of those, and the trigger-man disappears."

"So . . . wait. You think they aren't just killing bad guys, they're getting other bad guys to kill bad guys, and then killing *those* bad guys?" Laura sounded truly horrified, but I had to admit it was fiendishly logical.

"Hey, I know it sounds bad, but our stats look great. Crime's down across the board almost eighteen percent."

"Nick Berry!"

"I know, I know." He slumped against the steering wheel. Luckily he'd gotten off the highway and we were at a red light. "We gotta put a stop to it. Tell me something I wasn't the first to figure out. Why do you think the chief's been riding my ass?"

"The entire force should be out on this, not just you," Laura continued, snug in her cocoon of moral superiority. "It dishonors all of you. Your chief should understand that."

"The last thing we need is the papers getting ahold of this tidbit. So it's on the down low for now."

"You worry too much about the papers. Also, nobody says *down low* anymore," I announced.

Nick sighed. "Bad enough you have to come along. Next time," he said, catching my gaze in the rearview mirror, "Pollyanna stays home."

I shrugged. "See if *you* can make her."

We were in a fairly beat-up Minneapolis neighborhood, one of those places that might have been pretty a few decades ago, but had suffered from a few too many absentee landlords, and not quite enough good jobs.

Nick parked, and we all got out. The street was dimly lit, and clumps of teenagers and twenty-somethings stood out like mush-rooms sprouting on various corners. We got a few looks, but nobody came over — or appeared to recognize Nick as a cop.

The storefronts were all empty, some with windows soaped over. The sidewalks were a mess; paper, beer bottles, and cigarette butts all over the place. If I hadn't been dead (or with the devil's daughter), I never would have gotten out of the car.

At least it wasn't too cold out yet; it was nearly seventy degrees, not too shabby for nighttime in September. It was funny; I'd always had contempt for California and Florida transplants who bitched about how cold the weather got in my home state. Shoot, I used to wear shorts in February and sneer at the whiners.

That was all over with, now. *O, irony, you are a harsh mistress.* I actually had a pair of gloves in my Burberry handbag . . . how was *that* for wimpy?

"I've just got a tag number," Nick was say-ing, "but I don't know if it ties in to —"

I didn't hear the rest, because I was distracted by rapidly approaching footfalls and turned just in time to get slammed off my feet. The chilly sidewalk rushed up to smack into my back, and I cracked my head hard enough to see black roses.

Then someone with truly awful breath was yanking me off the ground by my purse strap, which, to my amazement, held. I had no idea if I was mad or glad. It *had* been a gift from Jessica. It was my only designer handbag. But then, if it had snapped free, I wouldn't have a stranger's hands around my neck right now. Decisions, decisions.

"Leave her alone!" Laura shrieked, while around her, teens fled. "Let her down! Detective Berry! Do something!"

"Freeze?" he suggested.

Bad Breath Boy and I were spinning around on the sidewalk in a tight little dance, and the stench of fresh, drying, and old blood was making me nuts.

"A Fiend," I managed, trying to break his grip — he was much taller, much broader. "It's a Fiend, don't get too close." Here? Now? What the *fuck?* Had they followed me from the house? Worse, had they followed Laura? That could be extremely awful.

"I could shoot it, but might kill Betsy by mistake. Ah, well," Nick said cheerfully, and I could hear him unsnap his holster. "A risk I'm willing — hey!"

There was a blinding light, like someone was holding a bolt of lightning, and then the light swung through both of us. It didn't do a thing to me but make me blink furiously.

But the effect was devastating on the Fiend, who didn't so much burst into flame as burst into ash. This was actually really weird for a vampire — unlike in the movies, where most vampires, when killed, just laid there, dead forever.

Not this one; he was a puddle of ash inside filthy clothes. Oddly, there was no smell, and no real flash of heat, just that blinding, gorgeous light. This made sense, as it wasn't *real* heat that had demolished the Fiend.

I coughed explosively, spitting dead Fiend out of my mouth and wiping it out of my eyes.

"Holy shit!" Nick said from the sidewalk where Laura had shoved him. "What the hell did you do?"

"*Hell* being the right word," I muttered, straightening out the kinks in my back, groaning and spitting. I was pretty sure Nick didn't know Laura was the spawn of Satan, so I kept the explanation brief, yet truthful. "That's her hellfire sword."

"You said that like 'that's her third cup of coffee.' "

"You know how some girls get pearls for their sweet sixteen? Laura's mom gave her weapons made of hellfire."

"You guys never tell me anything. I should have guessed your sister would be a freak like you," he bitched, climbing to his feet — only to get kicked over on his back by Laura, who was still holding her sword made of light.

"Now, Laura," I started, trying to swallow my nervousness.

"She was in trouble, and you just *stood* there," my sweet, good-natured, murderously dangerous sister hissed. "She might have been hurt or killed! Protect and serve, my ass!"

Uh-oh. She'd said *ass* instead of butt. Really mad, then.

"That was a Fiend! She said that was a Fiend! You *led us down here,* and a Fiend jumped her! Did you plan it? Do you have something up your sleeve besides catching rogue cops?" She jammed her sword under his chin, and his eyes watered at the light. It was pure bluff; her sword only disrupted unnatural magic: vampires, werewolves, spells. And only when she wanted them to, which is why it didn't work on me.

But Nick didn't know that.

"Get that thing out of my face," he snarled, not quite daring to bat it aside. "Think I would have brought a damn witness if I was trying to eighty-six your sister?

188

Or are you as dumb as you look?"

"Stop it, that's enough, just — quit!" I gently pulled my sister away. "Laura, put that thing away before half the street sees it."

Laura sullenly complied, sheathing her sword into . . . well, nothing, as far as I could tell. Nobody knew where her weapons went when she wasn't wreaking havoc with them.

"And you!" Nick, climbing to his feet, nearly fell over when I rounded on him. "She makes a good point, you know. A Fiend just *happens* to burst out of nowhere and try to kill me, and you just stand there?"

"What the fuck do I know about killing vampires? My bullets won't kill you. I don't think." The truth was, we didn't know. His bullets *had* killed a vampire . . . once. On my honeymoon, no less. "Why would they kill that thing? Do you think we have a police training course on arresting the undead? Do you think I've got Fiend Hunter tattooed on my forehead?"

"No, you've got Brutal Imbecile tattooed on your forehead," Laura interrupted.

"When I want your opinion, Barbie, I'll pull the string on your back."

"Give it a try," she snarled. "See how many fingers you pull back."

"You wanna go, Barbie? Because we'll go."

"Shut up!" I howled. "I'm not a queen, I'm not a wife, I'm not a big sister, I'm a WWF referee! Sorry, Nick. This expedition is *over*. Everyone get in the car *right now!*"

Meekly, they did. This was more like it — Eric and Tina never did a damned thing I asked them to. But first, Nick carefully eased my purse off my shoulder . . . I guessed he was going to try to get some fingerprints off it. We sure couldn't print the pile of ash on the sidewalk. I warned him not to use any of my credit cards and to leave the strawberry Blo-Pops alone. Sometimes I went through a dozen a day. It helped keep the blood craving down.

"Heir to the John Deere fortune, remember? I've got more money than *you* do, honey."

"Good. Then you can bring me to Wendy's," I commanded, all queen-like. "Being the victim of assault and battery gives me a craving for a chocolate shake."

CHAPTER 36

"That is strange," Sinclair admitted. After Wendy's, we'd ended up going back to the mansion and telling him and Tina what had happened. It was the first night of the full moon; Antonia was running around somewhere on all fours. Garrett had probably gone with her.

Jessica was visiting Marc at his new digs at The Grand, and I hoped he'd be able to come home soon. Things weren't the same without him. Besides, people disappearing out of our house brought back bad memories of last summer, when I was all alone.

Shoot, I even missed BabyJon's shitty diapers.

"Which part is strange?" Nick said dryly, bringing me back to my consideration of Sinclair's comment. "The part about my receiving a call and being sent to a bad neighborhood on what might have been a phony tip? The part where a Fiend just *hap-*

pened to run into us? Or the part where your wife's sister pulled a fucking flame brand out of thin air and killed said Fiend, before threatening to do the same thing to me?"

Hearing that Laura had threatened the officer didn't seem to perturb Sinclair one bit. "You say the chief is the one who gave you this assignment?"

"Yeah. And don't go there, pal, he's a stand-up guy."

"Oh, Nick." I shook my head sorrowfully. "Nobody says 'don't go there' anymore. Seriously. I'm so embarrassed for you right now. More so than usual, even."

He ignored me. "The chief's a year away from forced retirement — it's no time for him to fuck up a perfect record. It'd be the closest thing to suicide — this guy's job means *everything* to him. That's why Chief Hamlin wants these rogue cops caught, but he doesn't want to trash the police department's rep at the same time. Hell, he's the one who figured out the pattern — and the killings have been going on less than a month."

"I would think the reputation of his house would be the least of his problems," Tina ventured.

"Yeah? Come on, they're *still* making jokes

about the LAPD, and how many years ago was Rodney King?"

"Some might say," I said carefully, "that there've been one or two incidents in that department since the King videotape."

Laura beamed at me. "You're right, Betsy. Some police departments deserve the reputations they have."

I shrugged under Nick's withering stare. "I don't have a problem with cops," I said apologetically. "But I've been known to channel Jessica's point of view, from time to time."

"Getting back to the issue at hand," Sinclair suggested, "I wonder why this Fiend came alone. Did any of you get a look at which one it was?"

"Skippy," I said immediately.

"Skippy?" Nick asked, incredulous. "Friggin' Frankenstein was named Skippy? He was almost seven feet tall!"

I was embarrassed to hear the nickname repeated; what had at first sounded fun now seemed stupid, careless, and immature. Worse, nobody'd ever know the dead guy's real name now. The least I could have done when they came by was ask their real names. Mistake number 1,429 in what was turning into a shitty week.

"I am in your debt, Ms. Goodman, for the

assistance you rendered my wife."

Laura blushed to her eyebrows. "Oh, no, Eric, it's fine. We're family. I'm just happy *I* was there to help." She sharpened her words by narrowing her eyes at Nick.

"Hey, hey," he protested. "The whole thing happened in about two seconds. I could have got a shot off, but I might have blown a hole in your pretty wife's head. I mean, I could have lived with it, but —"

Sinclair silenced him with a wave of his kingly hand, which I could tell irritated Nick to no end.

"So what are you going to tell your boss? The chief?"

"That I couldn't find the tag, but I'll go back and look again."

"Alone," Sinclair said. We all noticed it wasn't a request. "You will go back and look again alone."

"You think I want those two PMS poster babies along for the ride? Ha!"

"Then allow me to escort you out," Tina said politely, getting up from the table.

"I'll see my own damned self out. In fact, I'm gonna start hanging out at The Grand instead of this house of freaks."

"The door can stick a bit," Tina yawned. "Make sure you pull it shut all the way behind you."

"Me-yow," I smirked as the door swung fully shut a few moments later.

Tina's bored expression vanished, nearly startling me into a yelp. "Curious."

"I was thinking the same thing."

"What?" I resisted the urge to yank my hair out by the double handful. "Oh, God, what now?"

"He insists the queen assist him in a delicate matter. He seems determined to put her in harm's way. He has made no secret of his contempt for and fear of her. And now, tonight — a Fiend happens to show up."

"You're not thinking — wait. What *are* you thinking?"

"But Nick couldn't be the rogue killer," Laura said — and thank goodness someone else was catching on. "He's the one killing all the bad guys, *and* he tells us all about it, and brings Betsy in to help him? You're saying it's an elaborate trap so he can kill her?"

"No way." I was shaking my head, though it did make a sneaky amount of sense. "He wouldn't dare."

"He does seem to dislike you a lot," my sister said thoughtfully.

"Yeah, but you guys are forgetting the Jessica factor. He wouldn't dare risk their relationship just to get me. I don't think he'd risk *anything* if it meant Jessica would toss him like hot vomit."

"An appealing image," Tina said, stifling a giggle. "But I still suggest we take a closer look at the good detective. A pity the body was essentially vaporized; I would love to have gotten his fingerprints."

"Why?"

"Knowing who they used to be would be helpful, I'm sure. If nothing else, Detective Nick could see if they had priors, when they were born — like that."

"Sorry," Laura said. "That's the trouble when hellfire meets vampire. Poof!"

"Yeah, it's cool, but then you've got dead vampire in your hair for hours. But Nick might have some luck with my purse. I'd better get that back from him, the crumb bum. Which reminds me, if the festivities are over for the night, I'm gonna shower."

"And I," Sinclair said, rising, "shall assist you."

He chased me all the way to our room.

CHAPTER 37

Sinclair was as good as his word; he soaped my back, washed my hair for me, and pretty soon we were groaning and biting each other under the pounding water. Sex in the shower didn't always work for people, but I was a tall girl.

And while he pushed, pushed, pushed into me, I watched the blood from my bite trickle down his back and swirl down the drain. Then the universe went away for a few seconds, while my orgasm took over my brain. Thank God Sinclair had a good grip, or I would have gone down like a sawed Sequoia.

We were relaxing in the second or third afterglow — we'd gone from the shower to the bed, and the sheets had completed the job of drying us — and I was grinning like a monkey. Sure, there were still problems, but now we were thinking about solutions. Maybe we were turning a corner on this.

Maybe we —

From far below us, the front door boomed open, and I heard the very distinctive sound of Antonia's growl, followed by Tina's shrieked, "Majesties!"

"It never ends," I moaned, reaching for a robe. Sinclair had slipped into a pair of pants and was already out the door. "It never ends!"

I beat him to the foyer, but only because he had too much dignity to vault the banister and bypass the stairs. Ha! Score one for — aggh! I had nearly skidded in the blood.

Antonia was in her werewolf form — I glanced at the bigass clock at the far end of the hall and saw that dawn was still at least ten minutes away.

She had dragged a dead Fiend in with her. "Um. Good dog?"

Garrett was shivering behind her. He clearly hadn't cared for the night's fun-filled activities, but knew he looked bad enough already in his lover's eyes.

I felt sorry for him. Anybody who says good guys never get scared and do stupid things has watched too many action movies. Yeah, he'd shown the less noble half of the human condition these past few days, but I could never forget what he'd gone through, and how far he'd come.

The man had never asked to become a vampire, or a Fiend, or anything else. He just woke up one day in a world full of pain, and wondered why. Just like the other Fiends.

I couldn't even look to myself as a better example of how to act. Any poise I had, I was sure, was a function of my ignorance of what I truly faced as queen. To put it more bluntly, I was so clueless about the magnitude of my new job, I was too dumb to be scared.

Antonia was sitting on her haunches, seeming to laugh at us with her wide mouth and eight zillion teeth. Her coat was the color of her hair, rich and dark. Interestingly, she had a white splotch on her chest, roughly diamond shaped. The splotch had a dark red smudge on it, and blood still trickled down her panting tongue.

Tina was examining the dead (again) Fiend. "This one appears to be the one Betsy named Sandy."

He was a large man, built like a farmer with thick shoulders and long, powerful legs. Not as tall as Skippy, but still formidable. Shirtless, with ripped jeans. No shoes or socks. His feet were filthy; God knew how long he'd been running around like that.

His throat had been torn out. Among

other things.

"She found his scent in the garbage pile out back — the stuff the contractors left after they fixed the house," Garrett said. "We've followed it all night. She caught him alone and — well. You can see."

"Sure can."

Okay, there was another corpse in my foyer, and that was, under any circumstances, bad. But Marc and Jessica were out, and untouched by this. So I was at a total loss as to how to react: Great job? Naughty werewolf? Thanks? Don't run off ever again on a murderous rampage, or I'll kick your ass? Murder bad? Murder good?

I finally settled on concern for my friend. "For crying out loud, Antonia! You could have been killed! Bad, bad werewolf!" I was towering over her, shaking my finger (but not getting it too close to all those teeth). "This is the sort of thing that can get you killed, and then where would Garrett be without you? You were really sweet to try and solve our problem, but I don't want you going off alone like that ever again!"

Bored, Antonia licked blood from her left paw.

"I mean it!"

The werewolf yawned.

"If you have more to add to your lecture,"

Sinclair said, his lips twitching, "you had better hurry. I estimate the sun will be up in less than five minutes."

"Dammit!" While I could withstand sunlight, the coming of dawn was still a narcoleptic trigger for me. Worse so than for other vampires; apparently, this was part of the price of being queen.

I tried to end my lecture quickly, but Sinclair had been (unintentionally, I'm sure!) mistaken: sunrise was in less than ten seconds.

"There she goes," Tina commented, as the floor rushed up to my face and everything went dark.

CHAPTER 38

Someone had considerately carried me up to bed (I prayed it was Sinclair), and I woke up with a large Post-it stuck to my forehead.

I snatched it away and read: *Developments! Come down as soon as you get rid of your horrible vampire breath. Also, your mom wants to know how long she's going to be stuck with BabyJon; I guess he's teething again.*

Oh, goody. Jessica was back. And my poor baby brother! He drooled like a beast when he popped a new tooth; I'd seen him soak an entire quilt. He was impossibly cute most of the time, with his shock of black hair, amazing blue eyes, and sweetly chubby limbs, but I could hardly bear to look at him when he was slobbering his way through the tooth of the week.

I couldn't help it; I grinned, picturing my mother's horror at watching BabyJon soak one of her antique quilts.

I hopped out of bed, shrugged out of yesterday's outfit, and brushed my teeth and hair. Then I changed into gray leggings, a dark blue PROPERTY OF RENFEST sweatshirt, and black flats — no socks. Then I hurried downstairs to the kitchen.

"— took him down so easy," Antonia was bragging. "Look! Not a mark on me."

"Anymore," Sinclair corrected her politely. "You don't fool *me,* dear."

"Okay, maybe El Fiendo got in a few good ones, I admit it. But I'm all healed up and *he's* roasting in hell. That puts it in the win column for me."

"It was foolish of the two of you to go after him by yourselves. You might have run into all of them."

All of them — I wondered how many were left. Jeez, even when I knew they were running around pissed at me, I couldn't keep track of them.

"Hey, think I'm gonna sit around on my ass while the fuckin' Fiends pop up without warning whenever they want? Who needs the pressure? Besides, I hate pop-ins. I hate this whole stupid situation." Except she appeared to be thriving on it.

"So where *is* the dead guy who was in our foyer?" I asked, gratefully accepting a glass of grapefruit juice from Tina. It wasn't nearly as good for me as Sinclair's blood, but I'd had enough from my husband to keep me going for a while. "Not that I mind that he's gone."

"The body," Sinclair said carefully, knowing how I felt about such icky things, "is in the basement, in the walk-in freezer."

I shuddered, and juice slopped over the rim of my glass. Among other things, when the mansion had been modernized thirty years ago, the old owners had put in a giant freezer for entertaining. Luckily, we kept it empty. Most of the time.

"We don't know if we will need access to the body again," Tina said apologetically. "I staked it after you fell asleep, just to be sure."

"Do we know his real name?" I wasn't expecting a good answer here, but I had to ask.

I got a pleasant surprise from Tina. "Nick was here, and printed him. He's going to run it through privately —"

"Why privately?"

Antonia gave me a "you poor dumb bitch" look, as Tina patiently explained, "What if the dead man was born in 1910? And he looks like a man in his late thirties? That might bring up questions we would find awkward to answer."

"Does Nick have enough juice to run prints — twice — without anybody else finding out?"

"We will see."

I had to be happy with that. I knew dick about police procedural. But if he was getting secret assignments from the chief, he probably had some clout.

"Thank you for your assistance, Antonia," Sinclair said over my musings. "We are grateful."

"Why do you think I beat feet to get back here from the Cape? You guys'd sit around and talk it to death. You need a werewolf to get shit done."

"Are all werewolves as insufferable as you are?" I asked sweetly, "or are you a genetic anomaly?"

Before she could answer, I looked around and said, "Hey, where's Laura? I'd think she'd want to be in on all this stuff now that she knows what's going on."

"She called while you were sleeping; she's teaching her church youth group tonight," Tina said with a barely repressed shudder.

"Okay, how about Jess? She left me a sticky note."

"You just missed her; she went to Detective Berry's house, complaining bitterly that it had been 'ages and ages' since they'd had some alone time."

"Why didn't she just go with him?"

"Oh, it's kind of dumb. She doesn't like to be stuck at anybody's house without a getaway car. It's one of her things. But it's great that she gets to see him tonight . . . he must have the night off."

Tina was opening her laptop. "Yes, yes, the poor deprived things. Let them stay gone for a month."

I was unwrapping a blue raspberry Blo-Pop. "Tina," I said reproachfully, then popped it into my mouth and sucked enthusiastically.

"Sorry, Majesty, you know I'm fond of Jessica. It's *him* I can't stand. And if he deliberately places you in harm's way once more, I may not be responsible for my actions."

"You shush. Just check your e-mail."

"Actually," she said, not looking up, "I'm checking Nick's e-mail."

I nearly gagged on the sucker. "Boo! Unless you've got a warrant. And vampires can't get warrants, I bet." I paused. "Can we?"

"You're so adorably naive, I may vomit," my husband said from behind the *Washington Post.*

"And you're so —" My cell phone chirped "Living Dead Girl" and I snatched at it. I

206

was sure it was my mom, bitching about baby duty. But there was no way BabyJon was coming back here until we — "Hi, Mom?"

"It's Jessica!" I winced and held the phone away from my ear. "You've got to come, quick! All of you! Nick's gone, but the Fiends have been here!"

"Whoa, whoa, calm down." I was trying to take my own advice and not hyperventilate. "How d'you know the Fiends took him?"

"Who *else* would break in and attack him? Please, please come right now! There's blood all over the place!"

"But — but —" I was so panicked I couldn't think, much less speak. "But why did they take Nick?"

"Because," Tina said, not looking up from her laptop, "the fingerprints came back. Forensics notified him by e-mail, but he hasn't actually gotten this message yet, so they had to move fast. And so will we."

"What? Why?"

"The Fiend's name was Edward Hamlin."

Hamlin? Why did I know that name? So much had been happening in a short time, I —

"Nick has been working on a little project for Police Chief Hamlin," Tina added, helping me out.

"We're coming!" I shrieked into the cell, then snapped it shut so hard I broke it.

CHAPTER 39

Nick lived in a great-looking bachelor pad in Minneapolis, overlooking the Mississippi River. The view was terrific, which made up for the fact that the yard was the size of a Post-it note, and just as yellow.

I'd never been there — luckily, Tina's laptop was stuffed with all sorts of interesting tidbits, including addresses she had no business knowing. She had MapQuested it, and here we all were.

Jessica had the place wide open for us, and I could see it was full of rich-guy toys: an extra truck, skis, a snowmobile, a Jetski. And that was just the garage. The house itself was brick, with dark green trim and a short, crack-free driveway.

Inside, the place was a complete shambles — we could practically follow the progress of the fight by observing the broken furniture and shattered glassware. He clearly hadn't gotten to his gun, which was too bad for him. I couldn't blame him — he'd been relaxing at home, getting ready for a date with Jessica, with no way of knowing his boss, the chief of police, had fed him to the wolves — almost literally.

Jessica was waiting for us in the living room, which looked like a bomb had detonated from beneath the carpet. He might not have had his gun, but he'd put up a helluva fight. It made me remember why I'd liked him a couple of years ago.

"Ballsy bastard," was Antonia's comment.

FALSE QUEEN was written on the biggest wall, the one without any windows. Sinclair leaned close, sniffed, then reported quietly, "Detective Berry's blood."

"But not so much that he's dead, right?" Jessica begged. "Not enough to kill him, right?"

Sinclair put an arm around my trembling friend. "No, dear one. Not nearly enough."

"She cannot go," Tina said firmly.

"Indeed, no."

"What are you two talking about?" I tried to keep my voice low and authoritative, when it wanted to go high and squeaky.

Tina shook her head, but Sinclair came right out with it. "This is an ancient challenge among vampires —"

"So how do Fiends who have been out of

it for six decades know anything about it?" I asked, trying not to sound hysterical.

"It's important to keep in mind they are remembering more and more every day — and in fact may have lied to us about what they *do* remember, at any rate." Sinclair glanced at the bloody letters again. "Regardless of how they know, they know. Such a step is usually taken to settle a grudge or, occasionally, determine ability to rule. This message means that if you value your crown, you will rescue Nick and defeat the Fiends."

"But how would I even know where to —"

"He'll be where it began for *them*," Garrett said quietly. I jumped; he hadn't said a word since we'd left the mansion.

"Nostro's house," Tina added.

"Well, then, I'm outta here!"

Cue huge squabble fest. Not even Jessica was sure I should go, and, needless to say, Tina and Sinclair weren't keen on the idea at all. Antonia was practically foaming at the mouth to come with me; she'd had a taste of Fiend already and didn't mind getting wet. I had a momentary flash — thank goodness Laura had her youth group tonight; she'd just be one more person trying to stop me.

Don't get me wrong, I sure as shit didn't want to go. I predicted a messy death and

Nick's curses being the last thing I ever heard in this life. But, like it (I didn't) or not, *I was the queen.* Did I think a hideous mistake had been made somewhere along the way? You bet. Was I going to welsh out of my obligation? Never in life. (Or death, I s'pose.)

The rules were, I go alone. So, I go alone. Besides, the Fiends would spot the others, and then they'd play kickball with Nick's head. How could I face my best friend if I got her lover killed 'cause I was too chickenshit to show up alone?

"— absolutely out of the question —"

"— but she's the only one who —"

"— can't leave Nick to —"

"— not open for discussion, as far as I am concerned —"

"— her responsibility —"

"— not going to let her essentially commit suicide —"

The argument was escalating in both intensity and volume (I noticed no one was much interested in *my* opinion), and there was no time, Goddammit, no time at all.

"Shut up, shut up, *shut the fuck up!* We have no time, don't you get it? Now I'm *going.*"

"Not at all," Sinclair said calmly.

"Tradition dictates she do exactly that,"

Tina said reluctantly, correcting her sovereign for maybe the fourth time in eighty years — a real toughie for her, since she wasn't too keen on me going in the first place.

"They'll kill you!" Jessica cried.

"Yes," Garrett said. "They will."

"The fuck they will! They can't take the king and queen *and* a fellow Fiend *and* me. We'll eat 'em for dinner! Let's go! Right now!" And I noticed an odd thing; all the fine hairs on Antonia's arms were standing straight up. If she'd been in her wolf form, she'd be bristling all over.

"We had practically the same group the first time the Fiends came, and we ran away," Jessica said. "What's changed?"

"A challenge written in your lover's blood," Sinclair said, kindly enough.

"Come on, you chickenshits!" Antonia barked. "We can take those fuckers."

"Maybe. And then Nick will be fish food," Tina said, biting her lip.

"My alpha's not going alone, and that's how it is!"

"Shut up, Antonia, all of you shut up! Just — shut up!" My head was pounding, like it was going to split down the middle of my forehead; I was clutching my temples and wondering why it was so damned hot in here. It seemed like the heat was battering at me, trying to get in, and all at once I dropped my hands and let it, let it all in, let it burn me alive.

Instantly, the room went quiet, a quiet broken by the thuds of my friend's bodies hitting the floor. I stood over them, shocked. Knelt quickly and found Jessica's pulse, realized Tina and Sinclair were as alive as they could be, just unconscious. Antonia, too, was out cold — and so was Garrett. I was the only one still standing.

And I felt like a million bucks. I felt like I could jump across the Mississippi. And I loved the sudden peace and quiet — I could finally hear myself think. I felt almost — what was the word? *Euphoric.* Yeah. I felt — I felt an awful lot like the way I'd felt when I'd sucked Marjorie dry, only not so frenzied and out of control.

I'd done it again! The chill in my bones subsided as I realized I had not killed anyone this time. In fact, they were safe and sleeping and, did I mention, *safe?* How did that work? Was it something I could control? If I didn't, what did?

I had no more time to think about it. If any of my friends woke up while I was still here, the trick I'd pulled (can I call it a "trick"?) would have been for nothing.

Knowing exactly where I had to go, I got the hell out of there, casting a last guilty look at my unconscious husband.

No sex tonight, that was for sure.

CHAPTER 40

After borrowing (okay, stealing) Sinclair's Lexus SUV, I made the trip in less than half an hour. Nostro's old digs were a combination of farm and what Jessica called a McMansion. Most of the houses in the neighborhood, while in the low seven-figure range, still looked a lot alike. They came with your standard pool, your standard half-acre backyard, your standard ballroom.

For an extra five figures, you could get either a gazebo, or a chicken coop. "Wholesome country living with the convenience of city living," that's what the brochure said. I knew, because my dad and the Ant had lived in one. It had been left to BabyJon, along with all their dough and the condo in Florida; some lawyer I'd only met once was keeping everything in a trust for him.

The McMansion was brown, with cream-colored fake shutters (what exactly was the point of shutters that didn't open or close, anyway?) and a big, crimson-colored front door. The walkway and patio were brick; the grass was starting to get a little shaggy. There was a tall hedge that went around the side of the house that I could see, and a few baby trees in the front yard. In a hundred years they'd be gorgeous elms. It was weird to think that I might be around to actually see that.

I brazenly parked on the front lawn (yeah, that's right, the queen of the vampires is here!), giving thanks that the nearest neighbor was on the other side of the lake.

I walked up the sidewalk and knocked on Nostro's front door, remembering the last time I'd been dragged through this very door. I'd been a vampire for about two days, no idea what was going on (as opposed to, you know, now), and almost before I knew it, people were bowing and calling me queen. It had been more bizarre than senior prom.

Nobody answered, so I tried the knob — unlocked. Ah, a welcoming killer mob. Good times.

I knew my way around a little, but proceeded cautiously. Frankly, tracking them in the bland-smelling house was pretty easy — even from a floor away I could smell their reek.

I passed a sitting room, a library, a bathroom, two bedrooms, and an office on the way. Unlike our mansion, the McMansion had much larger rooms (older houses tended to have tons of little rooms).

In fact, the place seemed too big and rather empty; there was dust on a lot of the tables and countertops. Of course, Alice had been the only one staying here . . . before she was killed and dismembered, the poor girl . . .

There weren't any paintings or pictures on the walls and, weirder, no books. No books anywhere. The bookcases held wine bottles and lamps that looked old-fashioned but operated on electricity. No magazines, even.

At least all the lights were on, which made the whole thing seem less scary — I don't know why. I sure as shit knew that things went bump in the night even *with* all the lights on.

The carpet was so thick in each room that my footsteps made no noise, but I didn't much care, because I wasn't trying to sneak in. Instead I walked straight into the upstairs living room and was greeted with, "Who the hell invited you, blondie?"

CHAPTER 41

I blinked, more than a little surprised. Mostly at the fact that there was an *upstairs* living room; I'd never seen that before. Just more proof of Nostro's essential nuttiness. And I'd had more pleasant greetings. Shoot, the IRS guy had been nicer.

Focus, Betsy!

A bloody and battered Nick was slumped in a dining room chair. There was a row of floor-to-ceiling windows behind him and, weirdly, three of them were open. There was quite the breeze whipping through the room — I guess the Fiends, used to living outside, didn't much notice the cold.

Then I remembered that they'd been kept outside all year round, like dogs you didn't mind having around but didn't want to spend much time with, either.

They ripped up anything they got near; it's not like they were aware enough to sleep in beds, or even on a carpeted floor. You're act-

ing like they were POWs and you were a Viet Cong!

Nick wasn't tied to the chair or anything — why would they? But he sure was pissed.

"Well, uh, they sort of did," I answered, gesturing to the Fiends. "Invited me, I mean."

"You just *had* to come and save the day, didn't you?"

"Alone," one of the Fiends said — it was Stephanie, and she wasn't bothering to hide her surprise. "She came alone."

"Of course I came! What, you think I'd stop for cocktails instead?" The Fiends stared at me, unblinking, while I bragged, "You have no idea who you're dealing with." Okay, to be fair to them, *I* had no idea who they were dealing with. "You think you can get what you want by grabbing my friend —"

"I'm not your friend," Nick whined.

"Fine, you grabbed my best friend's boyfriend, and now you think you're going to get what you want. But you don't even know what you want, do you?"

The Fiends looked at each other, while Nick, looking thoroughly disgusted to be there, rolled his eyes.

I examined them as closely as I could without making it obvious I was staring.

Happy, Jane, and Clara looked a little better — something in the eyes, I guess. They didn't seem as savage or as confused.

Wonder of wonders, although they didn't appear to have showered, they were at least wearing clean clothes. It occurred to me that the bedrooms in the McMansion probably still had dressers with clothes in them. And these guys had eventually fed enough, or remembered enough, to realize that.

Jane had long, dirty blond hair — it hung halfway down her back in greasy strings. Her mouth was a thin line, and her fingernails were filthy, but, incongruously with the rest of her, she had bright blue eyes, definitely her best feature.

Clara and Happy also had long hair but of course Happy, being a guy, towered over them both. He was one of those fellas who are so big they slump to try to look smaller, which only drew attention to his sheer bulk.

Happy had the tip-tilted eyes of an Asian American and would have been pretty good looking, if not for the hate-filled expression on his face. His jeans and shirt were clean, but he needed to wash the dried blood off his chin.

I wondered if anything was driving the Fiends now *besides* hate for me.

"Look, guys, let's talk about this. I think

there's been enough killing, don't you?"

"No," Happy said.

"Because this could get a lot worse, you know. Before it gets better."

"It will never be better," Clara — also known as Stephanie, but I wasn't going to let on — said sadly. "I thought maybe —" She cut herself off, and I knew why. Even now, she couldn't let on to what she had been up to earlier. She was as much a prisoner as Nick. "Not ever."

"Then what's your goal?"

"You must pay for what you've done," Jane said.

"Pay as in kill? I didn't kill you, I didn't make you vampires and starve you — I tried to *help* you. You know what your problem is? The one you really want to hurt is dead. Nostro's out of your reach, and you can't fucking stand it."

"Stated with Kissingerian diplomacy," Nick snarked.

"Quiet, Chair Boy. Look, I'll apologize again, okay?"

"No," Happy said.

"Then what do you want? You want to go back in time? Because that's the only way to — wait." I thought for a second. And then another one.

I thought about Jessica, and how much

she loved Nick. I thought about these Fiends, and the lives they had before they became my subjects — yes, my subjects. And even if the old king, Nostro, had done this to them, I was still responsible for them.

So what would a queen do, for her subjects? What kind of queen did I want to be?

"Okay. Let Nick go, and I'll stay, and you can have at me."

The three Fiends glanced at each other.

"Maim, kill, fold, spindle, mutilate. Whatever. Just let Nick go."

"You offer yourself in his place?" Stephanie/Clara seemed genuinely shocked by the offer.

"Yup."

"This is not a trick?"

"Uh, I don't think so."

"You are not setting a trap?"

I lifted my bare hands. "If this were a trap, wouldn't I have sprung it by now? I'm here alone. I'm not here to trick you. I don't want to kill you. I want you to get better. If the only way you can get better is to deal with me alone, then this is your chance. So what the hell are you waiting for?"

Happy moved in and sniffed the air around me. "You are serious."

I made an effort not to lean away from him; yeesh, he stank. "Yes."

"It may be painful."

"It might be." I tried not to shake. I tried to sound brave. I guess I didn't, though, because he almost smiled.

"We give you no guarantees," he warned. "We may come after your friend here, anyway, after you're gone."

I thought of Sinclair. "My friend," I sighed, "will be the least of your problems, if you kill me."

"We are afraid of no one. Not even our queen."

I shrugged. "Obviously not."

Happy looked over his stooped shoulders at the other two. They gave no sign, but he seemed to understand them anyway.

"We accept. Your friend can go."

"No fucking way!"

The four of us stared at Nick.

"Oh no you don't," he hollered, white-faced with blood loss. "You don't get to save me, no way, uh-uh. They kill me, and you feel like shit for, what is it? A thousand years? *That's* the way it's supposed to be. You're supposed to live with failure, not be the hero. Hear that? You're not the hero, Betsy Taylor! So hit the bricks! Get lost! Crawl back into your mansion basement and hide again!"

"He does not want to go," Happy observed after a short silence.

"Yeah, no shit."

"Are you sure you wish to take his place?"

"I'm having second thoughts," I admitted grimly.

"Perhaps he is not the friend to her we thought he was," Stephanie told the others.

"Damn right we're not friends!" Nick hollered.

"Will you stop screaming? And no," I sighed. "We used to be, sort of, but no, not anymore. But the offer still stands. Let him go, and I'll stick around, and we'll see what we'll see."

"I have doubts," Stephanie told her comrades. Aha! I silently congratulated myself for stopping Sinclair and Tina from killing her.

"What d'you mean?" Jane asked. Happy looked like he was wondering the same thing. Both of them had a little suspicion in their eyes, and I prayed Stephanie would be careful with her next words, so she wouldn't give herself away.

"She is not what we expected." Stephanie circled me and Nick. "Nothing about her. Not her friends, not those she calls her friends but are not —" She stopped and sniffed Nick, who made a batting motion at her with his hands, like he was shooing away a fly. "She is not the queen we thought. She is not smart, or powerful, or terrifying. Not like a real queen."

"More like a commoner," Happy added.

"Thanks?" I called out.

"She might help us," Stephanie added.

"How?" Jane asked, shaking tangled hair out of her face. "If she is not like a real queen, what can she give us?"

"We could start with your names," I suggested, still hoping to avoid hostilities. "I'd like to know them."

My request confused them, until Stephanie cleared her throat. "My name is Stephanie," she told me, as if for the first time.

Happy licked his lips. His tongue was weirdly long. "Richard," he finally said.

"Jane," the third one said.

Huh, I told myself. *Jane's name is actually Jane! What are the chances?*

Chapter 42

I took a shallow breath and let it out. Okay. Things were going — if not exactly well, at least it wasn't the disaster on wheels I'd been envisioning five minutes ago. Names were a good start. Now to keep the lines of communication open.

"Stephanie. Richard. Jane. I . . . well, I can't say it's wonderful to meet all of you, just like I know you weren't exactly thrilled about meeting me. But I can say I'm glad I've learned who you really are. I, uh, felt bad about the silly nicknames."

"You did?" Jane asked, open skepticism in her voice.

"Well, sure. See, I —"

"Don't be fooled!" Nick warned them. "She's got this annoying weird charm thing going on. It's hideous. Like head lice. Everything she touches turns to shit."

"Would that include Jessica?" I snapped.

"Well," he snarled, "she didn't have cancer

before she moved in with you and a bunch of other mutant bloodsucking freaks."

I didn't even want to respond to that. Emotionally exhausted, I sat on the arm of the couch next to him and waited to see what the Fiends would do.

And for the first time, I noticed Nick was bleeding — from the inside of his elbows, his neck. There were more serious cuts up and down his arms — from the fight at his house, I assumed. Maybe he'd rolled on some of the broken glass on the carpet? Maybe he'd —

Oh, God, his neck. They'd — they'd fed on him while waiting for me. His skin must still be crawling.

I imagine he felt raped and suddenly couldn't look at him.

"We have to deal with this one before we do anything else," Richard said, hauling Nick out of the chair. "They don't care for each other, so he's officially become useless."

"Useless?" Nick yelped, outraged.

"Hey, a minute ago you were ready to die just to make me feel like shit for the next thousand years. Now you're all mystified because you might be executed?"

"We should kill him," Richard decided.

"What about the queen?" Stephanie asked,

looking around nervously as if the queen's guard was going to burst out of the walls at any moment. Ha! If only. I could use a last-minute rescue. Dammit, why, *why* wasn't my life more like a movie?

Richard squinted at me, and I got a decidedly distrustful vibe from him. "We should kill her anyway."

Then I got a stroke of real luck. Nick tried to pull away from Richard and briefly succeeded, separating himself for a bare second from his supernaturally strong grasp. Quick as thought, I stood up, snatched Nick by the back of his neck and the seat of his pants, and tossed him out the bank of windows.

"You biiiiiiiitch," he yowled all the way down. Then, thank God, I heard him cursing as he thrashed around in the hedges.

"She lies!" Jane shrieked, and came at me.

CHAPTER 43

God, I was *so sick* of people just launching themselves at me without warning. Big-time rude, not to mention hell on my nerves. I backpedaled like mad, physically and verbally.

"I didn't do anything to —"

Her fist was a blur, and I took a teeth-rattling punch in the mouth, which wasn't fun at all, and threw an elbow into Richard's throat before he could do the same.

I chastised myself immediately: I was fighting like a human, but Fiends didn't need to breathe. He did cough and grab his throat, which I figured was good enough, so I turned my back on him, seized Jane by the hair, and spun her across the room.

Richard recovered faster than I expected. He delivered a blow to my right kidney, which *hurt* — oh, man, getting punched in the back was no fun at all — and then delivered a roundhouse kick to my left kidney, which hurt even more.

"You told us you would not try to trick us!" he seethed, hurting me some more with his fists. Kick, kick. Stomp. Best I could tell, Richard was apparently quite the kickboxing champion in his former life. "You swore!"

"I said," I gasped between blows, "that after Nick left . . . ooof . . . I would let you have at me. Feels like . . . ow, ow, oh God *ow!* . . . I'm keeping my end of the bargain. Shame . . . aggh! . . . you couldn't keep yours."

"My end of the bargain," he hissed in my ear, "is to survive. That's all you taught me to do."

The fire inside me kindled, and I felt a surge of power, as something made Richard stagger back. It didn't knock him unconscious, much less kill him, but it did give me enough space to get up and straighten myself to my full height.

And yes, I was still wearing my Marc Jacobs heels, which helped.

"Maybe you're not as good a student as you think." I couldn't help the disdain in my voice, though normally I tried not to sound like such a snob. What was wrong with this man? His queen had spared his life from the wrath of her husband, offered an apology, reached her hand out in friend-ship — and he had slapped it down?

What was wrong with him? *Who the fuck did he think he was?!*

My blood ran super-hot again, and he shrieked as if I had struck him. Again, he seemed too strong to suffer worse than a blow — or maybe the fact that he shared my blood spared him from the worst I had to offer — but it didn't matter. His kick-boxing career was over.

"On your knees!" I snarled at him. When he didn't move, I ignited my blood again — yes, I think I was controlling it now, at least somewhat — and *made* him get down. And I won't lie. I wouldn't deny it felt good to see him submit. To make him submit.

I turned long enough to ensure that Stephanie and Jane were not coming at me — they weren't, since they, too, were on their knees — and then I gave Richard my full attention again.

Nick's chair had been upturned in the fracas; I reached down and snapped a leg off the bottom. "You and I will come to terms of peace," I suggested, "or you will die." A dim thought that this wasn't exactly the best way to enforce peace was im-mediately shoved to the back of my brain.

Richard's body was beaten, but his eyes

were still full of defiance and distrust. "I see your true colors. No peace, my queen."

"My true colors. My true colors!" I felt my fangs spring from my gums and resisted the urge to bite him on the face. I raised the stake and brought it down faster than he could possibly move . . .

. . . right into his throat.

I don't know what made me miss his heart. Maybe it was poor aim — swinging a stake in lavender pumps is harder than it looks. Maybe the part of me that wanted him dead wasn't as strong as the part of me that just wanted him to shut the hell up.

Pulling the bloody stake from his throat, I turned to the others, who were still (willingly) on their knees. His body made a soft thump on the plush carpet behind me. Yes, he'd be out of action for hours. "And now, what to do with you two," I said grimly, hands on hips. Richard's black blood dripped slowly onto my — oh no! — Ann Taylor linen pants. I quickly rearranged the stake.

"I, um, think we should let her go," Stephanie managed with her head down.

"Perhaps there can be . . . forgiveness," Jane said, also not looking up.

"Maybe," I agreed. "I guess that'th up to each of you."

"What?"

"Never mind." This was no time to let the Fiends know that I lisped whenever my fangs came out. It wouldn't exactly strike terror in their heart of hearts.

I could hear the squeal of brakes outside the windows, familiar voices, the front door opening, and pounding footfalls.

"In the thort time we have left alone together," I suggested, "you two thould probably do everything you can to look ath — *as* — unthreatening as you possibly can." Thank God, my fangs were retracting. I was still pretty thirsty, but it would appear that the energy I'd gotten from my family, as well as from Richard, were keeping the worst of the pangs away. "Because if you think *I'm* bad? You should see my husband in action."

They swarmed into the room like a pack of wolverines. I relaxed, smiled at the first face I saw, and felt some of the fire leave my blood.

"Don't you bitches touch — oh." Antonia skidded to a halt, then nearly went sprawling, as Sinclair almost ran her down. "Oomph! Um, we're here to save you."

"Go save Nick," I suggested. "He's in the bushes on this side of the house."

"*You will pay for* — oh," Sinclair said,

straightening as he took in the three pros-
trate forms around me. The others piled in
behind him and did the same. "Hmm."

"Yeah, so, thanks for showing up, but I
took care of things. Pretty much. Of course,
in the last week you guys whittled down
their numbers for me. That was," I decided,
"a big help."

Tina and Antonia each nodded. Garrett,
hiding behind Antonia, swallowed with what
looked like a mixture of relief and lingering
fear. He tried a shy smile, and I smiled back.

"Stake 'em all!" Nick hollered, limping
through the doorway and waving his arms
like the Winter Carnival grand marshal.
"Betsy, too!"

Jessica rushed to Nick, clearly relieved that
he was unharmed (well, it was possible he
had a sprained ankle, and that was a helluva
scratch on his forehead . . . and he seemed
to be favoring the ribs on his left side . . .).

"Agreed," Sinclair said, sighing at the
three Fiends. "Well, not agreed about my
wife. But the others must die now. In fact,
it is long overdue."

"As you wish." Tina pulled out a thin
mahogany stake from somewhere within her
navy blue wool sweater and skirt set (truly
frightening efficiency), and stepped forward.

"Forget it!" I said, holding up my hands.

"We are going to be magnanimous in victory."

"Magnanimous equals pussy," Antonia commented.

"Again?" Tina whined. "We're going to let them live again?"

"Elizabeth, they are too dangerous to simply —"

"I didn't say we were going to set them free. They'll have to earn their freedom." I turned to the three Fiends — well, okay, the two that were conscious. "You had a grievance with me. You should have stuck with *me*. Had all seven of you done that, seven of you might be alive now. I'd like it if you three, at least, stayed alive. It's up to you."

"What —" Stephanie swallowed, then tried again. "What do we have to do?"

"You guys can be the queen's personal bodyguards and doers of annoying chores. Or I can leave the room, right now, and my husband and friends will chat with you. A *lot*. Until you have cavernous facial wounds." I tilted my head toward the exit and not coincidentally to the people who would stay behind. "Your choice."

"Pick the stake," Nick suggested, wiping streaks of blood from his face. God, that made me even hungrier. And wouldn't he just *shit*? "You don't want to spend the next thousand years doing that twit's dirty work." He turned to me. "You almost killed me, you numb fucking twat! Again!"

"I did not! I saved you."

"You threw me out a fucking window!" Nick was actually going purple with rage.

I tried to hide my amazement. Unlike occurs in the movies, Nick clearly hadn't suddenly forgiven me and been warmed by my selfless act. We weren't going to ride off into the sunset together (so to speak) and get Blizzards from Dairy Queen.

Frankly, I didn't get it. In the movies, when the heroine did something heroic and cool, everybody loved her at the end. Okay, I didn't *really* expect life to be like the movies . . . uh. That was maybe a lie.

"You are a menace, and if I could make it stick, I'd throw your ass in jail for the next hundred years."

"Nicholas J. Berry!" Jessica gasped. "What is the *matter* with you?"

"With me? You should have seen this psycho bitch in action."

"That is *enough,*" she snarled, hands on scrawny hips. "When are you going to get it through your head that Betsy isn't the cause of all your problems?"

I was frantically trying to signal to Jessica, making a slashing motion across my throat, the universal gesture for "shush!" Although it made me sad, I felt Nick's rage was a perfectly appropriate reaction to the evening's festivities. I appreciated Jessica sticking up for me — she always stuck up for me — but she didn't have all the facts.

He had been attacked. Again. Violated by vampires . . . again. I was amazed he hadn't gone fetal in the hedges.

"How many times do I have to say it," Jessica was saying. "How many times do you have to *see* it? She's a good guy!"

"No, Jess, it's okay, he —"

"She drinks blood, because she's dead," he said, spitting on the floor — spitting blood, I might add, and I was ashamed, because my fangs were out again. I didn't dare speak anymore; I didn't want him to know I wanted to drink and drink and drink. "She's a killer, and you know it."

"I love her, she's the sister I never got, and *you* know *that.*"

"Ah, perhaps we could, ah, step into another room and discuss, ah, the new terms for surrender," Tina said, because even the Fiends looked uncomfortable to be witnessing the lovers' quarrel.

"Or maybe you could talk about this later, when everybody's calmed down," I tried.

"Don't make me choose," Jessica warned,

ignoring us. For her, the only person in the room was Nick.

"I'm not making you choose. *I'm* choosing. We're done." He wiped his face again, and we all pretended not to notice how his hand shook and how he couldn't look at her.

"That's right," Jessica replied coolly. "We are."

And just like that — it was over. *They* were over. We could all practically hear the snap.

CHAPTER 44

Stephanie and Jane were sullen, but agreeable — apparently being the doers of the queen's scut work was more appealing than being staked.

I gave them permission to live on Nostro's property (by vampire law, when you killed a vampire all his stuff came to you, so technically, it was my property), and they agreed to be at my beck and call, as it were.

I'd probably put at least one of them to work in my nightclub, Scratch. Another vampire property that had come to me by law — long story. Actually, that wasn't true. I had killed another badass vampire, and her property went to me about the time her soul went shrieking into Hell.

Unlike their lives before, the Fiends wouldn't just frolic in the moonlight like undead puppies, but they'd live and read and watch TV like real people . . . which should be fun, since for all I knew Jane and

Stephanie had no idea what a TV was.

They could feed on each other — if they were comfortable with that — or they could snack on bad guys. We would help them figure out who it was all right to bite and who was off-limits. Yep, they could make new lives for themselves, be almost like normal people.

Unless I needed them, of course. Then they'd come on the run, or I'd know the reason why. Shit, with all the bad guys popping out of the woodwork these days, I *needed* bodyguards.

Of course, we weren't going to just leave them to their own devices . . . Sinclair and I would have to think about who could keep an eye on them, maybe even live in the Mc-Mansion with them. For now, they were cowed enough by recent events that I felt safe leaving them there for the next few nights.

"That was pretty anticlimactic," Antonia bitched on our way out.

"What can I say? It can't be bloody revenge and near-death experiences every day."

"You're about to have a near-death experience," Sinclair promised grimly as we climbed into his Lexus (I noticed Nick's truck was also there and deduced they'd

241

grabbed it when they woke up at his house after I'd put the whammy on them). "Specifically, you will never, ever sucker punch me like that again and run off into mortal danger."

"I didn't do it on purpose." Not quite a lie.

"Irrelevant."

"I'm not getting laid tonight, am I?"

"Probably not."

I batted my eyes. "What if I let you punish me?"

He paused, and his step actually faltered; I imagine he was thinking about my drawer full of scarves and our four-poster bed. Then he straightened up and went back to being Sir Pissypants. "Do not change the subject. You must promise to never, ever —"

"I won't!" Strangely, I felt my blood start to heat up again. *And I won't do that again, either. At least not right now.* Who knew if my friends could take it again? Besides, I really had no right to their — their life essence, maybe? Whatever it was that I could feed on without touching them. It wasn't mine. And I wasn't a thief.

With that in mind, I struggled to hold my temper, something I wasn't especially good at. "Sinclair, enough with the promises to stay safe and hidden from the world. It didn't suit me when I was alive, and I certainly can't comply now."

"I will not tolerate —"

"Are you listening, schmuck? You almost *died* this summer. Had I acted then like you wanted me to act this time, what would have happened? You'd be a pile of fucking ash, and you'd still be full of shit!"

"Aw, that's romantic," Antonia piped up.

"Damn right it is." I turned back to my idiot husband. "I love your arrogant ass, numbnuts, and I'm not going through something like this summer ever again. Besides, there are going to be times when we'll have to deal with problems alone . . . I mean, jeez. If *I* can figure that out, you can, too. You're just going to have to get used to the idea."

He sighed, and I could tell he wanted to smile at me but was forcing himself to remain stone-faced. The better to intimidate you with, my dear. Too bad it didn't work on me. Never had. "I love your arrogant ass as well, my own, but I meant every word I said, and you will mind me, Elizabeth. In this one thing, you will mind me."

"Fuck you, lover. I'm the queen, and I'll do as I please."

"I am the husband, and you will do as

you're told."

"Hi, I'm Betsy. Nice to meet you."

"Do not sass me."

"Do not piss me off."

He stomped his foot. Actually stomped it (clad in a Kenneth Cole loafer), like a kid having a tantrum. I managed not to laugh. Just barely. "This argument is over!"

I stomped my heel, nearly staggering — damned vampire strength! If I ruined these pumps I'd never forgive myself. "You're fucking right it is. Go suck on a turnip."

CHAPTER 45

We got out of the car, still not talking to each other. Even more awkward, Jessica and Nick had tagged along in his truck — I would have thought he'd had enough of me for a lifetime, but there wasn't room in Sinclair's SUV for me, Sinclair, Antonia, Garrett, *and* Jessica. Is there anything worse than being trapped in a car immediately after you've just broken up with your boyfriend? Eeesh.

Worst of all, the Ant was waiting for me on the porch, knockoff-clad toe tapping impatiently. "It's not over yet," she warned.

"Tell me about it," I snarled. "It'll never be over, until you cough up why you're sticking around." I walked through her, shivering (it was like walking through a curtain of freezing water) and opened our front door. "Why can't you go to hell like any other —"

Suddenly I was shoved so hard, I smacked

into the wall and fell down. The impact forced a shower of plaster to rain down on me. There was the deafening boom of a pistol being fired several times over my head. We were trapped in the doorway like ants in a straw — nobody had any room.

"That girl," a new voice said, "had amazing reflexes. I haven't missed a shot in forty-six years."

"Chief Hamlin?" Nick asked, horrified.

I slowly sat up. The Minneapolis police chief, less than a year from retirement, was standing at the end of the foyer, smoke curling up from the barrel of his pistol. He was a tall, gray-haired man in a neat dark blue suit, with wrinkles cutting deeply into his face, kind blue eyes, and a smoking gun.

"My father told me about you over three weeks ago," he said to (ulp) me. "How you left him for dead on that God-awful farm."

"Wh-what are you — ?"

"I was just a boy when he disappeared — and died the first time, best I can tell. By the time he came back years later — last month, in fact — I was a police chief."

"But I don't understand why you —"

He was staring at me with exhausted eyes. "You were all he could think of. He was the gentlest man I'd ever known, and all he could think of was hurting people. Hurting you."

"So you set him to work," Nick said shakily. "You sicced him on perps we couldn't put away. Pretended to figure out the pattern — which I bought, because you've got a great rep as a detective. Gave your dad cold guns, so we wouldn't think it was a vampire."

"But these guys had a caretaker at the farm/mansion place." I was having a terrible time puzzling this out. "She never noticed your dad kept slipping off the property?"

"Silly boy. They killed her a month ago."

That explained why Tina and Sinclair couldn't puzzle out Alice's remains. They hadn't been fresh. And it was entirely possible they *had* known and kept the info to themselves. It would be typical behavior. I bit the inside of my cheeks, so I wouldn't start shrieking at them.

Secrets, secrets. Cripes. My life was stuffed with them.

"Jeez, jeez," Nick was saying, his hand on his hip. I could see his fingers wanted to pluck at a gun he wasn't wearing. "Your only mistake was sending him to me when you gave me the fake tags to check."

Chief Hamlin shook his head. "I didn't send him. He had been following your

Betsy. And when he saw her on the street —"

"He snapped, and —" I almost said, "My sister killed him," but rapidly rephrased. I didn't want *any* of this fallout to poison Laura's life. "I killed him. But you didn't count on Nick getting his fingerprints off my purse strap. Once he had that info, it wouldn't have taken long until he knocked on your door."

The chief's lip trembled. "He was my father. He would not have hurt me."

I shook my head. "Oh, man, you're so wrong. Like, the earth is flat kind of wrong. I don't even know how to explain it to you. You don't understand what he had become."

"He was my father," the chief repeated. It was clear he was trying to convince himself, more than anyone else. "Back — miraculously — from the dead. And only I could help him." He shuddered at whatever memories of his father he had and looked past my shoulder. "A shame about your friend. I've never seen anyone move that fast in my life."

I didn't dare turn to find out whom he was talking about. "She'll be okay," I said bravely, hoping that was true. "And you won't get a second chance."

"No," he said politely. "She won't be okay. I used twenty-two longs, you see. But you're right about me. I won't get a second chance. I have only the one gun, you see — and by my count, one bullet left. I figured I'd never get the chance to reload, given the size of your entourage." He looked down at his gun. "I wish I had hit you and finished what my father started. I'll have to settle for hurting you. I hope your friend was important to you. Very, very important."

I still refused to turn around. Tears began to well in my eyes. "You're going to regret what you've done, asshole."

"No, I'm not. I have no intention of letting you turn me into what my father was."

Then he tucked the barrel under his chin and pulled the trigger.

Nobody tried to stop him. In fact, before his body hit the floor, I was already turning to find out who had taken the bullets meant for me.

CHAPTER 46

I first realized who it was when I saw the cascade of black waves blowing in the chill Minnesota wind — our front door was still open. The body lying face-down beneath that hair did not move.

Tina was lifting one pale hand, checking for a pulse. Garrett was holding the other.

"Why isn't she getting up?" I asked, rushing to Tina's side. "What kind of bullets were these? Were they silver?"

"They didn't have to be silver," Tina guessed as she examined Antonia's body. She knew more about guns than anyone I'd ever met. "Twenty-two longs, as he said, quite perfect for the job. They ricocheted around her skull but didn't exit. That particular ammunition lowers the innocent bystander rate. He may have expected civilians — or perhaps Detective Berry — to be near you when he shot you."

"But she's a werewolf!" I shook Sinclair's

comforting hand off my shoulder.

Tina looked up at me, eyes almost black with sympathy. "Her brains are all over the floor, Majesty. There will be no coming back from this."

I barely noticed Garrett get up and slip out of view.

"But she — she's Antonia!" Foulmouthed and smart and strong and invulnerable. And alive — always so vibrantly, shockingly alive. "She can't be — I mean, shot? It's such a mundane way for someone like her to —"

"No." Jessica staggered as if the shock was going to knock her on her ass, and Nick steadied her. "No, she can't be. You're wrong. She's not."

And the worst part was — "She jumped in front of me. She — saved me."

"Everybody saves you," Nick said neutrally. He tried to slip his arm around a sobbing Jessica, but she knocked it away.

Then we heard the splintering crash come from the stairwell.

I stood, trembling at the subsequent silence, and peered into the foyer. I choked back a sob at what Garrett had done to himself.

The regretful Fiend-turned-vampire had kicked the banister off a stretch of curved stairs in the foyer, leaving a dozen or so of the rails exposed and pointing up like spears. Then he had climbed to the second floor to a spot overlooking the stairs and swan dived onto the rails, which had gone through him like teeth.

"See?" the Ant said sadly as we stared down at the second body of a friend in less than a minute. "I warned you."

"Yeah, well." I wiped my face. "You could have been a lot more specific."

"I didn't know exactly. But I had a feeling. This stuff is pretty inevitable around you."

"Please go away."

"Yes, I think so. You wouldn't believe how depressing all this is. Good-bye, for now." And like that, she was gone.

"We'll take care of the bodies," my husband told me quietly.

Jessica kicked the wall and wiped tears from her cheeks. "Take care of the bodies? Just like that? It's not that easy, Eric. You can't just snap your fingers and make vampire minions clean up the crap. Not this time. What about Chief Hamlin? How are we going to explain *that?*"

"Don't worry about it," Nick said, clearly uncomfortable. "I can fix that."

"You can fix that," I spat. "Like you helped us fix things with the Fiends. Like you wanted me to fix your problems. You're going to fix this."

Sensing my lack of faith, he coughed and softened his tone. "Yeah. I can. I promise. Um, Betsy. You've had a rough — I mean, maybe you should, uh, go lie down."

"I agree," Sinclair said, too quickly. "Elizabeth, let us handle this for you."

I wanted to leave. God help me, I wanted to run away from this house and never, ever come back.

But I'd settle for fleeing to my bedroom and dropping the mess in my husband's lap. And the cop who hated me.

"It was all just so — so stupid," I said. *And preventable,* my conscience whispered. *If only you'd been paying attention to business . . .*

I trudged up the stairs. Nobody went with me, which suited me fine.

CHAPTER 47

Sinclair came upstairs hours later and cuddled me into his side. I sighed, and he stroked my shoulder and then kissed that same shoulder. I closed my eyes and breathed in his scent . . . warm, clean cotton. And dried blood, of course. Mustn't forget that. Not ever.

"She died well."

"I don't give a fuck. I want her back. I want her *here*."

"As do I, Elizabeth. But I will honor her memory forever, for the sacrifice she made. It might have been your brains all over the foyer."

"Well, what if it was? Why should I be alive and Antonia be so much cooling meat?"

"I do not know, dear one. But I am fervently glad it worked out the way it did, for all I was fond of Antonia."

I mulled that one over for a minute or two while Sinclair sat up, slipped off my shoes, and rubbed my feet. I wiggled my toes against his palms and almost smiled. Then felt bad for thinking it'd be okay to smile, even for a second.

"I just don't get it," I said at last.

"Get it?"

"When stuff this awful happens, you're supposed to learn something. Look Both Ways Before You Cross The Street. Be Kind To Children And Small Animals. Something. Jeez, anything. But there was all this death, all this waste, and for what?"

Sinclair was quiet for so long I assumed I'd stumped him, a rare and wonderful thing. But he was just trying to figure out how to break it to me. Should have known.

"It is that to be queen," he said at last. "There will be times when you will see an ocean of blood and despair. So it says in the Book of the Dead, and so it shall be, dear wife."

"You suck at cheering me up. You're not telling me there's gonna be worse days than *this?*" To say I was appalled would be putting it mildly. "What else did that rotten Book of the Dead tell you?"

He paused for a long time. Then: "Elizabeth, I can promise nothing, save that I will always be by your side."

I noticed he didn't answer the question.

"Oceans of blood," I said.

"Possibly. Yes."

"We'll just see about that."

"Elizabeth, if you'll forgive a pun, do not bite off more than you can chew."

"That's been the story of my life since I woke up in that funeral home wearing the Ant's shoes. Oceans of blood? Shit on that. Shit all *over* that."

I had no idea what I was going to do, or how. But I was going to work *real* hard to make sure my friends and I never had to go through a week like this again.

This was going to sound dumb, but the empty crib in the next room was practically calling my name. I had to stop fobbing my brother on other people.

I wondered if the Ant ever visited him.

CHAPTER 48

It was a day later; Garrett had been respectfully buried. Sinclair owned several farms and lots of land; what with Alice's remains, among others, we were starting quite the little private cemetery out on Route 19. It was awful and interesting at the same time.

The police chief's body had been found in his home, dead from an apparent suicide. Many cops went on record saying he had been deeply depressed about retiring but had rejected counseling.

Deeply depressed. Yeah. They didn't know the half of it.

"I have to tell Antonia's pack leader what happened. They deserve to know what happened to her, how she died. How she — how wonderful she was. I got the impression her pack never appreciated her, didn't you guys?"

They all nodded. Sure, we knew. Her ability to tell the future (and not turn into a wolf) had given all the other werewolves the creeps. They had been happy to see her go. And when I had "fixed" her, the fact that she hadn't rushed back home meant so much to me. She chose to stick it out with me.

I'd never get the chance to thank her. As far as a recall, I don't think I ever thanked her for anything.

My chest hitched once . . . twice . . . then settled. No, I was done crying for a while.

"Anyway, I want them all to know how she saved me. Hopefully they can guide us in how to treat . . . what's left of her."

Poor Antonia was in our basement freezer until I learned more about werewolf rituals for their dead. I wasn't looking forward to telling the boss werewolf that I'd gotten his pack member killed (Michael Wyndham had a wicked temper and a terrifying left cross), but it was something that had to be done.

Jessica didn't say anything, just poured herself another cup of tea. I'd told her my plan the night before in a lame attempt to distract her from breaking up with Nick. I felt tremendously guilty that she'd picked me over him. Of course, I would have felt a lot worse if she'd gone the other way.

Maybe someday they could patch things up. I'd see if I could do something about that. He'd been hurt and scared and said things he didn't mean. I had tried to explain it to Jessica last night, but had no idea if she really heard me. Maybe . . . in time . . .

But maybe it was for the best if they *never* got back together. It would sure cut down on the vampire attacks he had to endure . . . the price of admission when you hung out with the people in Monster Mansion. And I truly didn't know how much more Nick could endure. He seemed like a rubber band, stretched almost — but not quite — to the breaking point.

I shook my head, then noticed Marc was shaking his head. "I spend one Goddamn week in a hotel and then *this*." He was feeling as guilty as I was; he was convinced he could have done something for Antonia if he'd been here.

"Mathematically," Tina began gently, "given the age and abilities of our opponents, we got off rather lightly. And Garrett made his own choice. I —"

"That's enough," I said coldly, and Tina shut up.

"When?" my husband asked, mildly enough. "I'll need to clear my schedule."

"Tomorrow."

"As you wish."

"I'll come with, if you like," Laura offered.

She'd been agog all evening, listening to our tale of the awful events of the night earlier. "It's not trouble at all."

I was glad she had missed it (yay, church youth group!), to be honest. No telling what the body count would have been if she'd lost her temper. Or where the chief's bullets might have gone if he'd known who had really killed dear old dad. Just the thought of it gave me the willies.

In fact, it was safe to say that her temper was hanging over my head like a friggin' broadsword. Someday I was going to have to really sit down and figure out just what the deal was with the devil's daughter.

But not today. Not even this month. I was just so fucking tired.

"I'd be glad to come," my sister was continuing, eager to help. "I've got a Toys for Tots meeting, but it's no problem to postpone —"

"No, I need you to stay here and hold down the fort. And Tina — Richard, Stephanie, and Jane need looking after. Move them here while we're out of town, if that helps. Or *you* can move out to the McMansion until we get back. It's just temporary, until we can figure out something more permanent."

Tina nodded and jotted a note to herself

on the notepad she always kept nearby. "As you wish, Majesty."

"I'll keep BabyJon for you," Laura volunteered.

I smiled at my sister and shook my head, then turned to my husband. "Actually, I'd like to bring him to the Cape with us, if you don't mind. I've been spending too much time fobbing him off on other people, which is no good. I'm the only mother he's got now."

Sinclair tried to hide the wince (not a baby guy, my husband), but nodded. "As you like, Elizabeth. I do agree, we should probably get used to the idea of being" — he didn't quite gag on the word — *"parents."*

"A fine thing, my son being brought up by vampires," the Ant said.

"I suppose you're coming, too."

"Of course," my dead stepmother said, amused.

"That reminds me," I told my puzzled friends. "I figured it out. Why the Ant's here."

"To find a cure for bad dye jobs?" Jessica joked.

"Not hardly. See, she lived for making me miserable, she got off on setting my dad against his only kid, she loved irritating me in a thousand small ways."

"You make it sound as if that was my only purpose in life," the Ant sniffed.

"It was."

"What was?" Jessica asked.

I kept forgetting no one could hear her or see her but me. Lucky, lucky me. "Never mind. Point is, she's not done yet," I finished. "Not near done. So she's not going anywhere. She can't."

"Believe me, I've tried," she said sourly.

"So we're stuck with her indefinitely."

"That's right!" the Ant said triumphantly. "No more Mrs. Nice Guy!"

Exactly. Things were going to be very, very different from now on.

But the Ant didn't know me. Not the new me, the me that forced Fiends to their knees and broke necks and cured cancer. She was going to have her hands full.

For that matter, *anyone* who got in my way, who hurt my friends, who tried to stop me from making the world better, was going to have their hands full.

They didn't know this queen. Not like I did.

EPILOGUE

"You again."

"Me again," I agreed, plonking the six-pack of Budweiser into my grandpa's lap. He let out a yelp and gave me a look like he'd like to burn me alive. I'm sure if he'd had a can of gasoline and a box of matches, he would have tried.

He slipped a can free, popped the top, took a greedy swig, then let out a satisfied belch. "Ahhhh. You're not entirely useless."

"Aw, Grandpa. That gets me right here."

He grunted and almost smiled — almost. "Where's the new guy? The Injun you married?"

"It's Native American, you old jerk."

"Oh, fuck me and spare me that PC crap."

I could see we weren't going to get anywhere unless I worked around to my topic of conversation a lot faster.

"To answer, he's looking after his business and junk like that." Truth was, I had no interest in involving myself in Sinclair's business affairs. One, it would have bored me near to death. Two, he'd been making himself rich for decades. He sure didn't need any help from me.

I settled myself into the chair across from the bed. He was in his wheelchair (the one he didn't need) by the window. It had been full dark for half an hour.

"So what's on your brain, Betsy?"

"I distinctly remember you telling me on several occasions that I didn't have one," I teased gently.

"Yeah, well, you never come over without a purpose. Introducing the new guy. Telling me about that twat and your dad when they died. So what do you want? There's a *Sandford and Son* marathon starting in twenty minutes."

"How d'you do it?"

"Do *what?*" he said impatiently, then slurped up more beer.

"Kill people. And then not worry about it." I was speaking with a world war veteran, a man awarded the Bronze Star. Fourth highest award in the armed forces. It was hanging on the wall above my head.

His platoon had run into some bad luck, had been in the wrong place at the wrong time . . . a not unusual occurrence in

264

wartime, I was sure. Grandpa had grabbed his Lee Enfield sniper rifle, found scant cover, and picked off Germans one by one while his buddies were scrambling to get away. As sergeant, he had *ordered* them to get away.

He took four bullets: two in his left arm, one just above his right knee, and one had clipped off his left earlobe. Two of his men had dragged him away, as he protested bitterly that he was just fine, *fine, Goddammit, let go, you jackasses, I've got work to do!*

I had work to do, too.

Meanwhile, my grandpa had finished the beer (barf . . . words could not describe how much I hated the taste of beer) and was holding an unopened can in his left hand. "Kill people? Izzat what you said? And then not worry about it?"

"Yeah."

"What happened, idiot?"

I shook my head. "It's a really long story, and I come off pretty bad in it."

Grandpa shrugged, instantly losing interest in what brought me here, what had happened to make me ask that question. As Margaret Mitchell wrote about Scarlett O'Hara, he could not long endure any conversation that wasn't about him.

"It was wartime," he said at last. "They

were the bad guys. It wasn't like it is now. Things were a little more black and white back then. They were killing every Jew they could find. I think those little black beanie things the men wear are pretty stupid, but it's no reason to pick 'em off like God-damned mosquitoes."

I had to admit, I was surprised. Among other things, my darling maternal grand-father was a major bigot. I found it distinctly interesting that he'd fought because he saw a minority in trouble.

He was staring out the window now, and I had the very strong impression that if I spoke to him before he'd gotten all of it out, he'd clam up and take it to the grave.

The secret.

"Yup, they were doing terrible things," he mused. "And we were fools to wait until after Pearl Harbor to kick some ass. But once we were there, we were *there.* We did the work, and we didn't bitch about our feelings the whole time, either. God, I hate that 'tell me how that makes you feel' touchy-feely bullshit."

I nodded. I knew that, too.

"And when my guys got in a tight spot — why, I looked out for 'em just like they'd been looking out for me. I just kept that in my mind. Keeping my guys alive and sending as many of the bad guys to Hell that I could. That's all I thought about."

He looked straight at me, his eyes — my eyes — green and gleaming. "And then I never thought about it again. What for? Dead's dead, honey. You don't know that by now, I wash my hands of you."

"Thanks for the tolerance and acceptance," I said dryly. Thinking, *there's a trick or two I could tell you about death, Grandpa. Things you never, ever dreamed of. Things that would turn your hair white, if it wasn't already.*

But of course I wouldn't.

"What it comes down to is this, Betsy: you do what you need to, and then you haul ass out of there. Every single time."

"And never think of it again."

He nodded and popped the second Bud. "I didn't say it was an easy road. Shit, I lost plenty of my own fellas over there. I still miss Leary, that Irish fuck. But he died for a reason — a good one. Maybe the best one — kicking ass to keep the bullies out of the sandbox." He was looking at me almost sideways, a sly look. "So whether you killed somebody or someone got killed 'cause a you — oh, I can see it all over your face, girl, aren't you my own flesh and blood? Just . . . never think of it again. Life's messy, honey."

So's death, I thought, and turned the conversation to other things.

ABOUT THE AUTHOR

MaryJanice Davidson is the bestselling author of several books, most recently *Undead and Uneasy, Dead Over Heels,* and *Swimming Without a Net.* With her husband, Anthony Alongi, she also writes a series featuring a teen were-dragon named Jennifer Scales. She lives in Minneapolis with her husband and two children and is currently working on her next book. Visit her website at www.maryjanicedavidson.net or e-mail her at maryjanice@maryjanicedavidson.net.

The employees of Thorndike Press hope you have enjoyed this Large Print book. All our Thorndike and Wheeler Large Print titles are designed for easy reading, and all our books are made to last. Other Thorndike Press Large Print books are available at your library, through selected bookstores, or directly from us.

For information about titles, please call:
   (800) 223-1244

or visit our Web site at:
   http://gale.cengage.com/thorndike

To share your comments, please write:
   Publisher
   Thorndike Press
   295 Kennedy Memorial Drive
   Waterville, ME 04901